PETRUS BOREL

THE TREASURE
OF THE ARCUEIL CAVERN

&

GOTTFRIED WOLFGANG

TRANSLATED AND WITH AN INTRODUCTION BY

COLIN BOSWELL

THIS IS A SNUGGLY BOOK

ISBN: 978-1-64525-097-5

THE TREASURE
OF THE ARCUEIL CAVERN

"PETRUS BOREL" was the pseudonym of Joseph-Pierre Borel d'Hauterive (1809-1859), one of the most intriguing figures of the French Romantic movement. Born in Lyon, the twelfth of fourteen children of an ironmonger, he studied architecture in Paris before abandoning it for literature. Noted for his eccentricity and the extravagance of his writing, which was fully manifest in his masterpiece *Champavert, contes immoraux* (1833), his work is today viewed as a precursor to Surrealism.

COLIN BOSWELL studied French Language and Literature at University College London. Whilst completing a PhD he began his career lecturing in French at Goldsmiths University of London and later at the University of Kent, where he was also Development Director. He then created and served as Executive Director of the first European office of the US-based Council for Advancement and Support of Education (CASE). He has published books and articles on the French language and on Émile Zola, and his translations include Gustave Kahn's *The Mad King* for Snuggly Books.

CONTENTS

INTRODUCTION

ACCORDING to Enoch Powell, a twentieth-century right-wing English politician, all political careers end in failure. It could be argued that the same is true of the literary careers of geniuses, with that of the nineteenth century French writer Petrus Borel being no exception. In the 1830s Borel, the self-styled lycanthrope or man-wolf, was a major figure of the French Romantic movement. He played a leading role in a number of prominent writers' groups and was looked up to by writers such a Théophile Gautier and Gérard de Nerval. These writers were active after the July Revolution of 1830 which saw the overthrow of Charles X and his replacement by Louis-Philippe, Roi des Français, and which created a bourgeois, materialistic society that they hated. It may be this society, allied to the outbreak of cholera in 1832, that is referred to at the end of the first chapter of *The Treasure of the Arcueil Cavern* in which Borel tells us that the tale may distract us from "more real misfortunes".

But by 1845, with his literary career going nowhere, he applied to the Ministry for Colonisation for a post as Inspector of Colonisation in Algeria, arriving there on 25 January 1846. After a satisfactory beginning as a colonial administrator, he eventually fell out with his superiors, became involved in litigation against the Sous-Préfêt that he could not and did not win, and was dismissed in August 1855. He continued to live in Algeria, where he died, possibly of sunstroke, on 17 July 1859.

Borel was born in 1809, the twelfth of fourteen children. He was educated in Paris in Catholic seminaries and, according to the critic Enid Starkie,[1] this gave rise to violent atheism and anti-clericalism. It is the case that in *The Treasure of the Arcueil Cavern* the priest, Le Père Bacheville, cuts a rather sorry figure. After school Borel initially trained as an architect and this may explain the detailed architectural description of the interior of the vault containing the treasure in Arcueil. But according to

---

1 Enid Starkie, *Petrus Borel The Lycanthrope. His Life and Times*, London, Faber and Faber, 1953.

Starkie "even as a schoolboy Petrus Borel had already acquired that passion for collecting scraps of learning which was later to develop into vain erudition and pedantry."[1] Some of this is arguably evident in *The Treasure of the Arcueil Cavern*. But by 1829 Borel had decided to abandon architecture and devote himself entirely to literature. According to reports he played a major role in the now famous "battle" of *Hernani* in 1830, where Victor Hugo had recruited a claque to ensure the success of his new and convention-breaking play.

In 1833 Borel published arguably his most important work, *Champavert, Contes Immoraux*. *Champavert* is made up of five short stories, two of which have links to the two stories in the present volume. In *Monsieur de l'Argentière* there is the execution by guillotine of a woman found guilty of infanticide, giving a foretaste of *Gottfried Wolfgang*. In another story, *L'Anatomiste*, an old doctor of anatomy, Don Andrea Vesalius, who has married a younger bride, finds that he is impotent with her. He therefore allows her to take lovers. But each of these lovers mysteriously disappears after one night of passion. It is later revealed that Vesalius has had the lovers killed and used

1 Op. cit. p.22

their bodies for anatomical experiments. We can link the description of the bodies to the preservation of the two corpses in *The Treasure of the Arcueil Cavern*. Unfortunately for Borel *Champavert* was not a financial success.

But, despite his lack of personal literary success, he was not without influence. "Petrus Borel was the kind of meteoric personality who is thrown up by violent revolution, whose light burns brightly for a short space, as long as the fashion for destruction prevails, and then finally, because he cannot adapt himself to the conditions of stable society, splutters out into obscurity. He was, by nature and inclination, capable of destruction, but he never learned to build. Yet his stormy passage has not been in vain, for he hewed out a rough channel which later writers—Baudelaire, Rimbaud and Lautréamont—have deepened for the greater glory of literature, and who owe much to him, who might indeed never have existed had it not been for his fulgent example."[1]

According to Starkie by 1842 "All his former companions had reached some measure of success and security. Petrus Borel alone was like a sailor stranded on some desert island from which all his comrades had sailed away."[2] Again

1 Op. cit. p.193
2 Op. cit. p.145

in the words of Starkie: "At this time he was also writing a considerable number of short, and probably ill-paid, articles for various papers: for *Le Commerce*, *Le Journal des Chasseurs*, *La Sylphide* and *La Revue de Paris*. Only two stories that he wrote at this time are worthy of notice; these are *Le Trésor de la Caverne d'Arcueil* which appeared in *La Revue de Paris* in April 1843 and *Gottfried Wolfgang* which came out in *La Sylphide* in the same year."[1]

Our two stories, *The Treasure of the Arcueil Cavern* and *Gottfried Wolfgang*, vary considerably in length. The first is almost a novella whereas the second is a truly short, short story. But they share an interest in the occult, including satanism in *The Treasure of the Arcueil Cavern*, and an evil genius in *Gottfried Wolfgang*. Starkie sees *Gottfried Wolfgang* as a tale that Edgar Allen Poe might have written.[2] It also appears to have impressed Alexandre Dumas who plagiarised it in his own *La Femme au Collier de Velours* published in 1850. In both *The Treasure in the Arcueil Cavern* and *Gottfried Wolfgang* feminine beauty is idealised, as we see in Brederode's descriptions of Suzanne de la Filandière in *The Treasure of the Arcueil Cavern* and of the unnamed woman in *Gottfried Wolfgang*. It is not

1 Op. cit. p.145
2 Op. cit. p.145

11

important but interesting to note that the story proper in both tales begins with a character crossing the Place de Grève in Paris.

The main theme of *The Treasure of the Arcueil Cavern* is, as the title states, hidden treasure and as we are told in the story, "nothing is more attractive to the human mind than the story of riches mysteriously hidden underground." He refers in the story to the widespread belief that the Moors, as they retreated from Spain, had left behind hidden treasure. In England there is a widespread belief that in 1216 the baggage train containing the treasure of Bad King John, whilst crossing the estuary on the east coast known as The Wash, had been engulfed by the incoming tide. More than eight hundred years later people are still hoping to find this treasure and there is at least one person who thinks they know where it is.

Had Borel lived in the twentieth century he would have witnessed the happenings at the southern French village of Rennes-le-Château where curious stories began to circulate about a nineteenth-century priest, l'Abbé Saunière, and some of his financial activities. Amongst other stories about him, it was alleged that Saunière had discovered the residue of a treasure of

28,500,000 gold pieces that Blanche de Castille had assembled as a ransom for Louis IX who had been captured during a Crusade. This and other stories about Saunière, including the study *The Holy Blood and the Holy Grail*, led to 100,000 visitors a year visiting the village, mostly inspired by Dan Brown's *The Da Vinci Code*.

The motivation for "money for nothing" which inspires our seekers after the Arcueil treasure is similar to that of the millions of people around the world who weekly "invest" their pound, dollar, euro, etc. in their national lottery in the hope of winning a life-changing fortune.

In both stories Borel decided not to use a third person omniscient narrator in the same way that Mérimée did later in 1845 with *Carmen*. In *Gottfried Wolfgang* the narrator of the "outer story", possibly Borel, is merely retelling a story found amongst the papers of an unnamed Englishman who we assume had committed suicide by jumping from the jetty in Boulogne. But the question of whether the author of the "inner" story is the Englishman himself or whether it is a transcription or a translation of a German story that he has found, is left unresolved.

Borel's narrative technique in *The Treasure of the Arcueil Cavern* is even more complex. Narrator (1) who tops and tails the narrative and who intervenes occasionally during the story to reassure us that he is faithfully reporting, almost verbatim, Count Brederode's tale, seems to be Borel himself since he signs the story off with his own name. But the main narrator, Narrator (2), is the Dutchman Count Brederode who, as a prisoner in the jails of Vincennes and the Bastille, tells the main part of the story to his fellow prisoners. But Narrator (1) does not tell us how he came by the story of Narrator (2). According to Narrator (1), Narrator (2) died early in the eighteenth century, therefore their lives did not overlap. Did Narrator (1) get the story from Brederode's fellow prisoners? If so, when and how?

As a narrator Brederode is rather engaging with a sense of whimsy. He is also very erudite, although whether this becomes the "vain erudition and pedantry" referred to above by Starkie we will leave the reader to judge. But there is a major part of the story that Brederode cannot have been aware of. He was, after all, already in captivity when, as a result of Bacheville's accidental fall, the underground vault and treasure is finally discovered as well as the notebook belonging to Adolphus which reveals the innermost secret of the story. Therefore, here we seem to have Narrator (3) and possibly Narrator (4)—if we count the notebook of Adolphus as Narrator (4). How did our main narrator, Brederode, Narrator (2), come by these stories? But maybe this is just the nit-picking of a twenty-first century mind and we should just allow ourselves to be taken along by the flow of a "ripping yarn".

Clearly the work of Petrus Borel is not part of the canon of major nineteenth-century French literature. In the words of Enid Starkie: "Posterity, on the whole, has not treated Petrus Borel kindly, nor has it ever given him his just deserts, whereas it has singled out for special praise many a lesser writer. He is now almost forgotten, except amongst a small number of devotees who find the by-ways of literature often more absorbing than the highways."[1] We hope that the readers of *The Treasure of the Arcueil Cavern* and *Gottfried Wolfgang* will find these two by-ways both absorbing and enjoyable.

---

1 Op. cit. p.193

I would like to thank my wife Sue Boswell for her extremely valuable comments on an earlier version of this translation and to Brendan Connell, for his always helpful advice and skilful editing. Any imperfections that remain are, of course, entirely my responsibility.

—Colin Boswell

THE TREASURE
OF THE ARCUEIL CAVERN

I

AT the beginning of the last century there was in the Bastille[1] a young man who said he was Dutch, enjoyed the title of Count, and claimed to belong to the famous house of the Marquis de Brederode, Lords of Vianen, close to Utrecht.

Every time his fellow prisoners asked him why he was there, the sole reply this mysterious character gave was the strange story that will unfold below.

Did he wish to disguise the real reason for his imprisonment behind a fable? Had a long and cruel detention made him mad? Was he telling the truth, even though the story was scarcely probable, or was this adventure only something imagined by his mad brain? No one

---

1 The infamous Parisian prison, the storming of which on 14 July 1789 marked the start of the French Revolution.

knows—I do not know the answer—and no doubt the answer will never be known.

Even the archives of the Bastille only contain the date of an inmate's arrival and the date of his release; and without what a few prisoners who heard his secrets have told us, and who, more blessed than him, saw an end to their misfortune, this victim of a crime that was certainly less serious than the punishment would have remained completely unknown.

Just imagine this! To be born—to be twenty years old—to be thrown into a cell—to die there—without leaving behind even the mark of a footstep or the sound of a complaint! . . . Imagine! To suffer and to tell oneself:—"For me posterity will shed no tears and will not re-examine the judgment of my judges! Can there be in the world a more atrocious fate?"

But let us quickly turn our minds away from such gloomy thoughts. Without further ado let us come to the strange story or rather the dream that our prisoner recounted, and let us try like him, using very strange, even imaginary, ones, to forget more real misfortunes.

We are going to allow Brederode to speak for himself for fear of altering in any way the simplicity and originality of his account, and he normally expressed himself as follows:

II

ONE evening, I am not quite sure what hour had just rung from the parish church of Saint-Gervais, I was crossing the Place de Grève,[1] and as I was arriving at one of the corners of the square suddenly from an inn close by a booming voice called out to me.

"Hey! My friend! . . . Count, a word or two! Please come and join us!"

I hesitated for a few seconds and then accepted this sudden invitation.

Who on earth is calling out to me here? . . . "Ah! It's you, reverend father!" I cried.

---

1 Now the Place de l'Hôtel de Ville in Paris. It is on the banks of the River Seine and takes its name from *grève* [tr. as "shore"]. It was a place where people looking for casual work congregated, unloading boats. Later it became a place where workers would come to protest about their working conditions. It gives rise to the expressions *"une grève"* ["strike"] and *"faire la grève"* or *être en grève"* ["to be on strike"].

I had noticed sitting at table, in front of a few bottles, a monk who had recently become an acquaintance of mine and who, as convention demands, was as flourishing as it was possible to be and comfortably plump.

"Welcome my dear friend," said the monk, "please do us the honour of sharing a glass with us. Just try, I beg you, this cheeky little wine from Aquitaine. Come on now, do not stand on ceremony. Let us drink and say glory to the Lord!—And speaking of our Lord, are you afraid of the devil?"

"No, reverend father."

"You are not afraid of the devil! God be praised! You are a real man! Let us fill our glasses and drink a toast to the devil's health!"

"That goes too far, reverend father; it is certain that I am not afraid of the devil, but that does not mean that I like him. You raise a glass to his prosperity if you want to; I shall refrain."

"Are you really not afraid of the devil?"

"Reverend father, I have already assured you that I am not."

"Ah! So much the better! For I want to make your fortune for you," replied the monk lowering his voice and affecting an air of benevolence.

"Make my fortune! . . . Thank you, father, you really are a decent fellow, for these days it is not easy to make a fortune without going off to the Indies to preach the Holy Scripture."

"Listen to me, my dear count; I am being totally serious. We are planning to steal a treasure hidden in a cavern at Arcueil[1]. Everything is ready to carry out the plan successfully this very evening, be in no doubt. Come, if you dare, and you will share with us the enormous wealth of the treasure."

"Really reverend father! But this is an old and well-known story," I said with a smile, for I wanted to make fun of the monk and of his confidence. "A long time ago I heard about the treasure hidden away in the Arcueil cavern. I think you are a little late with your plan for the bird has already flown the nest."

"The bird has flown the nest! Certainly not, your information is not correct, my young friend; and with the devil's help, believe you me, we will find the whole brood in the nest."

"With the devil's help! To be frank with you, reverend father, I really do not see how and why Satan should come into possession of this treasure, and even less how, having command over it, he would be stupid enough to hand it over on the orders of a simple priest or a fortune-teller."

---

1 A township to the South of Paris, 5.3 km or 3.3 miles from the city centre.

"Just come with us, dear Count," the prior replied again calmly, for our monk who had renounced legal and military careers and had taken holy orders in order to purify himself through suffering on earth, nevertheless possessed a rich priory in Normandy. "Just come with us; be firm and resolute, and tomorrow you will have no further doubts about the reality of occult powers."

"But who is the priest, the sorcerer, or the exorcist?" I asked the holy man, to make fun of his credulity rather than out of genuine interest.

"But it is I, the exorcist priest, I, dear Count, your very humble servant and father in God. Where the magician is concerned, you will have a big surprise. When you meet him, you will be amazed . . . Look, here he comes. Indeed, he is arriving just on cue rather like a character in a play."

And indeed, a young girl, accompanied by several men of motley appearance, was arriving just at that moment.

"Well done, well done, gentlemen," he said to them; "I compliment you; you are men of your word." Then he added, pointing in my direction:

"I have the pleasure, gentlemen, of introducing to you a new companion, Count

Brederode, a Dutch aristocrat, who deigns to honour me with his friendship. Gentlemen, you can trust him just as you trust me; he is a good and brave gentleman, as faithful as his sword. You, young lady, come here and meet the Count," continued the prior, taking the young girl by the hand. "And you, Sir," he murmured in my ear, "pay homage to the terrible necromancer."

"Terrible!" I repeated, opening my eyes wide and weighing up the beautiful unknown lady. No, on my honour, such an attractive, such a talented young woman, far from inspiring feelings of terror in me, would rather inspire gentle feelings in my heart, and certainly I would consider myself really fortunate to have dealings with such a ravishing Circe.[1]

"Suzanne, dear Count, makes the devil tremble as you will soon see."

"If he trembles, the old miscreant, I wager that it is rather from emotion," I replied.

Then turning to Suzanne:

"Please tell me my beautiful child," I said to her, "who has taught you so well in devilment and witchcraft?"

"This knowledge, Sir, is hereditary in our family; my father was the most skilful sorcerer

---

1 An enchantress in Greek mythology noted for her knowledge of herbs and potions.

in the Landes[1]. Although he was only a simple shepherd, a hundred times he made the moon come down to Earth and got the sun to dance."

"Strewth,[2]" I cried, "this, my dove, has a whiff of the Garonne[3] about it. Nevertheless, without being too nosy, I would readily pay ten gold louis to know, my beautiful enchantress, exactly how the moon came down, and to know the exact tune of the minuet danced by the sun."

But, without giving me time to pursue my joke, the prior got me to take the hand of the young magician and invited me, along with the rest of the company, to move into the rear room of the inn, where a tasty and copious supper was served to us.

The good monk was not without credit with the hostess and, moreover, it was only, he said, a down payment taken in advance from the inheritance of the great treasure waiting for us in the grotto at Arcueil.

---

1 A region of South West France.
2 The oath "Sandis" in the text appears to be a euphemistic blasphemous Gascon oath meaning literally "the blood of God". We are grateful to the French author Arnaud Rykner for his help tracking down this etymology.
3 A major river in South West France, flowing through both Toulouse and Bordeaux.

III

THE meal was highly enjoyable. No expense was spared, especially on the wine; but that scoundrel, when you overindulge in him, does not spare you: he soon turned upside down that human reason of which we are so proud. When I say upside down, I am speaking hypothetically and I am presupposing, which is certainly very debatable, that it is normally the right way up. But the power of wine is really something quite wonderful! It is capable in the blink of an eye of changing us in an instant from being the most superb lion into a donkey. A Homeric genius that would dominate all geniuses, a Cartesian[1] reason which would surpass all reasons, you can destroy them with

---

1 René Descartes (1596-1650) was an influential French philosopher, famous for his sentence Lat. *Cogito ergo sum.* ["I think therefore I am"]. The Cartesian method is still held in high esteem in France.

a jug of grape juice. With six sous of spirits, you take away all logic from Blaise Pascal,[1] and for a small crown's worth of mead or maraschino you turn an elegant M. Regnard[2] into a dog stretched out in front of a door.

But let us come back to our sorcerers, who seem to us amiable and full of that gaiety that comes from the wine cellar, as we have just said. The conversation had heated up; it was a deafening noise, a genuine disorder.

"It's agreed then," shouted one, "that we will all have equal shares."

"In truth," said another, "if the treasure is as huge as we have been told, and if each person's share is enormous, I really don't see, upon my word, what I'll be able to do with mine."

"It's not difficult," replied the prior for my benefit, "I don't see a problem. I would use it . . . let me see . . . to build a chapel . . . or rather a delightful convent, that I will fill with virginal and well-chosen nuns. And as the director and founder it goes without saying that I shall have privileged access."

---

1 Blaise Pascal (1623-1662) was an influential French mathematician and theologian.
2 Jean-François Regnard (1655-1709), along with Molière, one of the great comic poets of the French seventeenth century.

"I strongly approve of this delightful plan and I would gladly imitate it, reverend father, were I not a layman," I said in order to take part in this general folly which was really beginning to entertain me.

"That's a fine difficulty to have, my friend!" the good monk replied again. "You are a layman; go off to Syria and build a harem."

"Your fertile brain is full of ideas, dear and venerable prior; but I thank you," I replied cheerfully; "I don't like the Turks and they are not keen on papists, these savage heathens who allow themselves to treat so roughly anything that falls into their hands. Really, I am not like that partridge who simply wishes to be roasted, or the saddle of hare asking to be cooked on a spit, as illustrated in the *Cuisinier royal.*[1] And as for you, father Le Bègue," I continued, turning towards a small character with a very odd appearance who until then had been silent and whom I had just recognised as a famous musician from Saint-Roch;[2] "come on, tell us I beg you, what will you do with your share?"

"What will I do with it, gentlemen!" retorted the fellow quickly with all the energy given

1 *Le cuisinier royal et bourgeois,* [*The Royal and bourgeois cook*] by François Massaliot (1660-1733).
2 A church in one of the most fashionable districts of Paris.

by a fine meal and addressing the assembly which quickly quietened down to hear his reply. "What shall I do with it! I shall immediately hand in my notice to the King; I shall say to him: 'Sire, I am tired of your company; find another organist.' Then, instead of founding, like you, nunneries or harems, I shall have a huge concert hall built, with a marvellous display of organ pipes, to which everybody would be admitted without charge, just as in former times the Romans were admitted to the circus; then I shall found a conservatoire[1] like those that have existed for a long time in Italy, something that is sadly lacking in our poor France . . . Alas, gentlemen, music is disappearing! The Flemish school is dead! The fine tradition of Lully[2] is fading day by day! Scarcely now would you find two good singers in Picardy, my homeland, in Picardy, where the whole of Europe, where Rome and Naples, less than a century ago, would come to find their talented musicians, just as today one goes looking for cod on the Great Banks of Newfoundland!"

---

1 Borel uses the Italian word *conservatorio* in the French text.
2 Jean-Baptiste Lully (1632-1687), an Italian French composer who worked principally at the court of Louis XIV.

This strange recantation was greeted with unanimous laughter, with everyone telling Father Le Bègue that his brain was as crazy as his organ pipes, that he was mad.

The unruliest were shouting: "Long live displays of food from the pantry! Down with displays of organ pipes!" And included in this number was our monk with the loud voice and the red chubby face.

"As far as I am concerned, gentlemen," I told them, "have faith in Count Brederode; I consider you all to be triple and quadruple madmen! And I care so little for the fortune, which inspires me with no confidence at all, that if it did so happen that I received fifty thousand louis as my share I would immediately spend twenty thousand louis on buying incense, myrrh and cinnamon, and another thirty thousand buying cedarwood and sandalwood and I would have it all transported in triumph to the middle of the Saint-Denis plain,[1] in order to prove at least once, by setting fire to it, the truth of the misleading and vulgar saying that wealth, like glory, is nothing more than vain smoke."[2]

---

1 To the North of Paris.
2 It is possible that Brederode is referring to a quotation by Rivarol (1753-1801): *"La gloire n'est que fumée, j'en conviens, mais l'homme n'est que poussière."* ["Glory is only

"Ah, straightaway, forgive us for being blunt with you, but it is you, Count, who have lost your marbles!" they all shouted at me from all directions.

My comic proposal had created the effect that I hoped for: it had brought the merriment to a peak.

I let the first features of this hilarity pass by and then, when the noise had calmed down sufficiently for me to be able to get a few words in, I undertook very calmly to prove to our boisterous companions that it was rather they than I who had gone mad, using as my final proof to them that it was only madmen who would count their chickens before they were hatched.

---

smoke, I agree, but man is nothing more than dust".] One of the most frequently quoted epigrams of Rivarol concerns the clarity of the French language: *Ce qui n'est pas clair, n'est pas français.* ["If it is not clear, then it is not French".] If Brederode really is quoting Rivarol he is guilty of an anachronism since Rivarol's life (1753-1801) comes after his incarceration in the Bastille.

IV

A FTER this wise remark that I had adroit-
ly made so that our fellow guests would
feel that they were indulging themselves just
as Hannibal's soldiers had in the delights of
Capua,[1] the prior immediately had coaches
brought forward into which the whole noisy
company rapidly climbed and installed themselves, each according to his affinities and liking. As for me, I attached myself to my friend
the monk, rather as a child does to the petticoat
of his nurse. Amidst these unknowns and this
darkness, he was my column of light.

After a rather long and rather painful journey, with absolutely no memorable aspects, our
modern Argonauts[2] finally arrived in Arcueil.

1 Hannibal had made Capua his winter quarters in 215
BCE.
2 In Greek mythology they accompanied Jason in his
quest for the Golden Fleece.

An accomplice, who had been secretly posted in the countryside and who was keeping watch, came immediately to meet us, and having let us in to the mysterious enclosure, led us to the hiding place of the so-called treasure. The hiding place of the treasure was, it goes without saying, a dark cavern; what would a cavern be were it not dark? Just as what would a traitor be if he did not look unpleasant and treacherous?

Now, whilst Suzanne, the sweet magician, was getting undressed; why was she getting undressed? I don't know: there seems to be a general belief that clothes, which are something unnatural, paralyse magic spells, since we see the most scrupulous writers with the highest reputations describe their necromancers doing this;—whilst, as I said, Suzanne was getting undressed, wishing to play the man of courage and composure, with a candle in my left hand and a sword in the right, I bravely went into the cavern and began to roam around in all directions without meeting anything, not even an owl.

Then Suzanne came in. All she was wearing was a simple little skirt trimmed with fine lace . . . Ah! The appetising little sorceress! She was carrying a resin torch and a wide-open book of spells.

With one other man from the group, I was then posted to the cavern entrance; the rest of the company was ordered to stay further away.

My companion and I had only been listening for a few moments when suddenly we heard Suzanne talking and shouting in a very imperious manner:

"You have broken your promise lots of times! I desire, I insist, I order you to hand the treasure over to me immediately."

On hearing this order, a voice that could certainly only have been the voice of an evil spirit, replied:

"Tonight, you will not be able to overcome my resistance, don't bother me anymore, there are too many of you; and if your companion, the priest, or anyone else takes it into his head to break the law I am imposing, I swear I will strangle him before you."

Hearing this strange utterance, I let out a great peal of laughter which echoed for a long time in the cavern. Was it a sincere laugh? Today I would not dare either to believe it or to uphold it, for this whole nocturnal contrivance was not without having made some impression on my mind. There would be odds of ten to one that I was silently trembling, as

Montaigne[1] said, in the citadel of my doublet. My henchman seemed petrified.

"Strangle him in my presence! No, no, I don't fear you," replied Suzanne; "I know how to stop you."

"Well then!" cried the mysterious voice, "tremble on your own account."

The devil, as he uttered this last threat, started, without the slightest respect for her beauty, to hit Suzanne violently. You could hear the blows resounding from her pretty body as clearly as we can hear from here the town clock chiming. It was simply heart-breaking!

As a true knight I wanted to fly to the defence of the beautiful underdog, but my companion held me back, swearing by heaven and earth that I would be lost if I took a single step.

Soon Suzanne reappeared, wild-eyed, bruised, dishevelled, and yet the courageous child did not cry out once.

The whole company had gathered around her and everyone quickly wanted to ask her a question: "What about the treasure, and the devil, mademoiselle?"

As for me I had reverted to my sardonic tone and I joked with the prior on the brilliant outcome of his expedition.

1 Michel de Montaigne (1533-1592), philosopher and essayist.

"Reverend Father," I said to him, "was it not agreed that the treasure, in other words what the devil would give up after the magic words of our young Hecate,[1] would be shared in a similar way and that each one of us would have an equal right? So, let us dispense justice.—Come on, Suzanne, come on, without pity, distribute the dividend to each one of us. Please give me the blows to which I am entitled."

But the prior was still putting on a good front; he settled for replying to this sarcasm with his usual candour:

"The devil, good Sir, is not as accommodating as you seem to think. Do not laugh like that. Next time we will have a better chance."

And just as we were withdrawing and getting into the coaches to head back to town, Suzanne proposed that we should make another attempt the next day and her proposal was accepted on the spot.

---

1 The goddess of magic and spells.

V

AND the following day, as agreed, all our gold-seekers gathered again at the cabaret de la Grève where we dined very cheerfully and again at the expense of our future treasure. Then at the time agreed for our departure we set off for the country house, the theatre of our shady investigations, belonging to someone in high society.

There, by the light of a full moon, on tiptoes and in silence, dead on half-past eleven, we went into the garden where Suzanne, who had sworn to the owner that we were alone in this enclosure, posted us individually as sentries at various distances one from the other; then she drew magic circles around each one of us and specifically ordered us not to step out of these mysterious rings.

As midnight sounded the young magician climbed up onto a raised mound, almost in the middle of all the sentries and unfastening her long hair she let it float down onto her beautiful shoulders. Then modestly she took off all her clothes, this time only leaving on the shoulder strap of her delicate lace petticoat.

Her slim, ravishing body, illuminated and dappled by the silver rays of the moon, was set against the tufts of bladder senna just like Francesco Albani's *Lovers*[1] set against green branches. Oh! It was ravishing! It had overtones of antiquity and of the time of the druids that . . . Ah! Suzanne, Suzanne, it was you who were harbouring the precious treasure.

When once again I saw the poor child in this simple outfit, I cried out to her from inside my magic circle, for I had not abandoned my role as a cynic: "Hey there, my beauty, but a breastplate would suit you better! Take care, you know that the devil did not pull his punches in the cavern."

As soon as there was silence again, Suzanne took her book of spells; she made frenzied

---

1 A reference to a series of four paintings by Francesco Albani (1578-1660) entitled *History of Venus*. Borel is probably referring to the painting entitled *Les Amours désarmés* [*The disarmed Lovers*] in which, unsettled by the triumph of Venus, her rival, the goddess Diana, silently presides over the disarmament of the Cupids who have been drugged by the nymphs. The painting is in the collection of the Musée du Louvre.

movements, she mumbled strange and barbaric words, no doubt in one of those unknown languages used in enchanted lands, such as those mastered by M. Lemaistre de Sacy and M. d'Herbelot.[1]

However, not fully content with these first spells, she skilfully opened a vein and tracing, with a drop of blood, a few letters on an oak leaf, she threw it in the air, letting out a strange shout to the sky.

Upon this dramatic cry, suddenly five magnificent horsemen, or rather five ghosts dressed in purple, white, blue, black and yellow, appeared in the air and came to prance above her head, like a prismatic reflection that a child enjoys making flutter on a wall. Suddenly appearing to fly up to them, to our great stupefaction, Suzanne soon disappeared.

I have no idea what these aerial phantoms could be nor where they came from nor where they took her; but what I do know is that the absence of our magician stretched on and on, and that each person was starting to get really bored at his post.

---

1 Louis-Isaac Lemaistre de Sacy (1613-1684) was a theologian and humanist whose translation of the Bible was the most widespread French Bible of the eighteenth century. Barthélemy d'Herbelot (1625-1695) was a French orientalist.

"Ye Gods, by Saint Waast[1] my patron saint, reverend Father," I said to the prior, "are we going to spend the whole night as if we were trees? We would finish by growing suckers and becoming bushy-leafed. What are we waiting for? Do you not see, gentlemen, that it is a conjuring trick! Whilst we stay here moping like fools, I bet ten gold coins that our beauty is resting on a fine feather bed chortling with laughter as she thinks of us. If we are not allowed out of our circle at least, reverend Father, may we lie down? For my amusement I would like to listen to the grass grow."

"Shush! Count; shush! You are blaspheming!" our monk cried out excitedly and as loud as he could. "Gentlemen, gentlemen, stay where you are; I beg you not to move or else you will be dead!"

But fortunately, the five rainbow-coloured horsemen suddenly reappeared, galloping at full speed up in the ethereal empire, and at the same moment a whirlwind of clouds, or something like it, brought Suzanne back, who fell precisely on the hillock from where, a short time before, she had been miraculously abducted, or at least seemed to have been.

1Vedast or Vedastus, Saint Vaast or Saint Waast was a Frankish bishop who died in about 540. Saint Waast is also a commune in Northern France.

In a dying voice she called out for help. With my sword in my hand, followed by the rest of our number, I rushed to her assistance. But a surgeon would have been more useful than a knight.

The poor girl was in a terrible state difficult to describe; her whole body was lacerated and ripped apart, her eyes were staring and full of tears, and seemed fixed at the back of their orbits. We had to carry her hastily to a sort of deserted hovel, situated in the remotest part of the park where, I was told later, she remained several days fighting for her life.

When I saw Suzanne in this awful state, I went up to the monk and said to him severely: "That is enough, Sir, I am giving up my entitlement to a share of the treasure. You are aware of my lack of interest in riches; what I was doing was really only out of curiosity; but my heart could no longer take part in the tortures of this unfortunate child."

"Good Lord! You must be joking dear Count," our fellow replied graciously, taking in my exclamation with his customary smile. "This accident is nothing. Believe me, I am telling you this in confidence, and only you, the devil has given his word that at the next full moon he would hand over the treasure."

VI

WHEN he reached this point in his story M. de Brederode would normally ask the prisoner listening to him, or sometimes the large audience that had gathered around him on their walks in the keep or on the gallery of the Bastille, whether, before he pushed on further towards what he called the final twist of his misfortunes, he should describe in a few words what the treasure in the cavern at Arcueil really was, or rather what was the origin of this old and widespread belief.

Nothing is more attractive to the human mind than the story of riches mysteriously hidden underground, especially to the mind of a poor man, for in these items that are hidden from our gaze only by a stone or a few handfuls of dust and which chance may reveal to anyone, he sees the unique solution that could rescue him from his troubles.

The peasant obsessed by financial needs never digs his spade into his poor and stony field without bending forward and listening out to check whether there was not some audible noise from the shock of his shovel.

The more a people have become poverty-stricken, the more important becomes the widespread idea of the marvellous existence of hidden treasures. From Murviedro to the Algarve, from Toledo to Grenada, there is not a Spaniard in a moth-eaten cloak, with neither pockets nor coins, who is not counting on the imminent discovery of one of the huge treasures that were hidden by the departing Moors in the foundations of buildings and under riverbeds. If one could turn our town over as one turns over a *tortilla* (an omelette) the good folk of Salamanca never stopped saying, one would find more gold than the New World has ever supplied or will supply in the future.

M. de Brederode's companions in misfortune enthusiastically greeted his seductive proposal. Could such a digression not only add to the pleasure they naturally got from his interesting tale?

It is true that our young Dutch gentleman had a special persuasive power when he allowed his imagination and speech to roam. You quickly left behind with him the sad domain of the real, something very agreeable for poor people in captivity; you quickly broke through your shell and, like the butterfly deploying his brightly coloured wings, you went away to stroll and flutter, far away from bolts and discipline, in a life full of fantasy and caprice.

When M. de Brederode had thus had his new itinerary sketched out for him by his listener or by his audience, he would then begin in his cutting and mocking voice, which was able to give importance to the most trivial items, the smallest detail, the sort of narrative that follows. In the same way as what has come before, we have made it our duty to make not a single change either in the content or the style of the story, for fear of substituting glacial reason and narrow draperies of a modern mind for the frills and the frank jokes of an older mind.

But let M. de Brederode speak for himself.

"In history as in grammar," he would continue, "everything has its etymology. Whether well-known or hidden, there is no belief, no matter how absurd it might seem, that does not have its source somewhere. As far as the existence of a treasure hidden in the cavern at Arcueil is concerned, since you wish to allow me to tell you, here is that clear and positive fact which, despite many counter arguments, was the origin of this widespread opinion."

VII

IN the final years of the reign of good King Henri IV,[1] at least that is how the story goes, there lived in Paris an old goldsmith who had a great reputation for the intricacies of his trade and for many other things besides, as was common knowledge at the time.

His house, of some repute but of quite sad appearance, was in a sort of square or hollow, behind the buildings of the old Louvre, and consisted of a wall giving on to the street, painted a curious green, with only one single narrow opening by way of an entrance, which made it look like a money box, something with which indeed it had several other similarities.

In earlier times there had been a pair of casement windows, but for reasons that you

---

1 Henri IV was the first Bourbon King of France. Born in 1589, he was assassinated on 14 May 1610.

will easily deduce from what follows, they had been solidly closed by strips of plaster. Poets do no less to the eyes of love.

Above the door, and this was the only external object which allowed one to suspect what was traded in this place, there was, nailed to a piece of wood, an embossed copper basin at the bottom of which could be seen through the rust a heraldic escutcheon, with the following inscription in a foreign language and characters: *Gold ist gut* (gold is good).

You may see from this motto that Master Jean d'Anspach, crown jeweller, was certainly not a hypocrite, that he was unaware or pretended to be completely unaware of today's vulgar art of blushing at one's own feelings; for if this man had a major fault (alas! who amongst us is beyond reproach?) it was that he was rather too fond of the material that he worked.

Some time ago, in his youth, he had come from the margraviate of Anspach,[1] his native country, with his leather tool bag and his simple companion's apron. But the skill he had acquired in Germany in carrying out incrus-

---

1 The principality or margraviate of Ansbach was centred on the Franconian city of Ansbach and was ruled over by Hohenzollern princes. Ansbach is south-west of Nuremberg.

tations and niello[1] on precious metals quickly made him a fashionable workman, the jeweller to the King and to the court.

Hardworking and sober, our German quite rapidly acquired a reasonable fortune which gradually, added to his strong desire to make a profit, ended up becoming for the time and for him personally, truly immense.

It is certain that amid all his happiness, he had been exceptionally miserly; it is also certain that he had sold, as he was entitled to do, expensively fine jewels to the King for his mistresses, and to the mistresses for their lovers. But no matter the depth of his parsimony, no matter the number of rings, pendants, caskets, jewel cases he had sold for Jacqueline de Bueil, for the delectable Mme Gabrielle or for Mme de Verneuil,[2] his wealth would never have reached its prodigious size if he had not mixed in with his normal work certain secret and underground financial operations, of a more dubious morality, such as pawnbroking and lending money at twenty per cent interest. His shop had been the battlefield where many inheritances in the making had been cut down;

1 An incrustation on engraved precious metals.
2 Jacqueline de Bueil, Gabrielle d'Estrées and Catherine de Verneuil were three of the favourite mistresses of Henri IV.

it was there that the young nobility had lost the flower of their fortune, if not the flower of their rank.

In a word, since sometimes one must call a spade a spade, Master Jean d'Anspach was one of those foul creatures spoken of by La Bruyère,[1] covered in mud and filth, smitten with profit and money-making, as fine souls are with virtue and glory.

It is often the case that people do not see even the most well-deserved happiness descend on the roof of their neighbour without a slight feeling of envy, and for those badly treated by good fortune, that sort of blind, stupid half-goddess, better suited to serving oats in a hostelry than to dispensing comfort to humans, it is their lot to cheer themselves up at the expense of those on whom fortune has so stupidly decided to smile.

Our man left himself wide-open to mockery. His unbelievable, unparalleled, incalculable avarice provided public malice with the most agreeable and fertile theme, on which common tongues never stopped wagging.

He was accused of not marrying for reasons of economy and of having frequently said that

---

1 Jean de la Bruyère (1645-1696) was best known for his satirical pen portraits published in 1688 as *Les Caractères* [tr. as *The Characters*].

he might well have taken a partner if he had been able to find a woman like Lot's wife, transformed into a pillar of salt, in order to have a bit more taste in his soup and also to defraud the gabelle.[1]

It was claimed, if I can really believe this, and truly I am embarrassed to explain this honestly to you that, when he sat down, for fear of wearing out the most important part of that most necessary of garments, he would generally roll his knee-breeches down round his ankles, and thus used to climb up naked onto the oak bench of his worktable, as the Numidian horsemen did on their wild horses if ancient history is to be believed.

A thousand more things were imagined, more or less cruel or comic; but these two profoundly characteristic traits should be enough for us, I think, to judge the extent of such enormous miserliness, many strands of which we have still to disentangle.

Master Jean d'Anspach, plunging his hands again and again into his treasure chests, casting wary looks at his own shadow, barricading his cupboards and bolting his doors, had passed many busy days when he finally began to realise that concurrently with his riches, he had

---

1 The gabelle was a hugely unpopular tax on salt that had been introduced in France in the fourteenth century.

also accumulated a significant number of years. He said to himself: "It is not enough to know how to acquire wealth, you must know how to preserve it; and indeed, now that I am less vigilant and energetic than I used to be, there is no safety in living any longer in such an insecure house built carelessly right on a public highway. To take a profit from our still being a going concern, let us not wait until our clientele, decimated each day by the scythe of time and death, have completely disappeared into their tombs, but instead let us retire to a more propitious place where we will finally be able to enjoy with leisure and security the precious fruit of our assiduity and hard work." As a result, he had sold his goldsmith's workshop at a doubtless very acceptable price and had gone off to incubate his spoils some distance away in a fine stately home in Arcueil that he had owned for some time.

As a result of interest piled upon interest, with renewals and respites, this property had passed into the hands of a poor noblewoman burdened with debt after the death of her husband, and who used the house as collateral to receive a modest pension.

Where the jewellery business is concerned, it would certainly have been more decent of the uncle to leave it to a young nephew, the orphan child of a sister, sent by wise tutors to Paris on the pretence of some sort of study so that he would be closer to the rich inheritance that awaited him. But Master Jean d'Anspach was not moved by ties of blood.

Far from it, he treated with boredom and mistrust the young man who was scarcely likely to arouse bad temper or umbrage. He would gladly have encouraged him to return to Germany or rather preferred to slam the door in his face; but the innocent young man, with his amiable, carefree, cheerful personality, slithered and wriggled like an eel amidst the evil wishes and acts of his uncle, without really minding or even paying attention. And whereas everyone around him told him that Master Jean d'Anspach was an evil, detestable human being, he simply smiled and said that he found the fellow eccentric.

VIII

ONCE he had moved and settled into his house in Arcueil, Master Jean barricaded himself in like a consul in Cairo during an outbreak of plague. Some windows had their closed shutters sealed; others were so well barricaded with iron that they looked more like Saint Laurent's grill[1] than windows. A small spyhole with a thick, narrow grating was made in a panel of the main entrance so that one could reply to whoever was knocking without opening the door. At the end of each path a snare was dug in and armed, and shards of glass and broken bottles were placed like chevaux de frise[2] on the tops of the walls.

---

1 Saint Laurent of Rome was an early Christian martyr who was executed by being burned alive on a grill.
2 In mediaeval warfare *chevaux de frise* were stakes driven obliquely into the ground and were used to impede the advance of cavalry.

And there you have the amusing and pastoral atmosphere that our old goldsmith, Master Jean the Miser, as the people in Paris called him, had managed to create in his comfortable abode. And once he thought he had managed to make himself sufficiently isolated, he immersed himself in the most absolute solitude, breaking, so to speak, with all human creatures and habits.

This new type of lord of the manor, as you can easily imagine, was not without creating a lively sensation in the district. As you well know, in a village the slightest event always produces the effect of a coconut amongst monkeys. But what really increased astonishment and brought to its highest point the general curiosity that had already been so strongly awakened, was the arrival of a dozen German workmen that Master Jean had brought at great expense from Anspach.

The men had spent several months housed inside the castle, and during their stay a large amount of stone and plaster had been brought in, sufficient to construct a large building.

Naturally, everyone expected to see rise, as if by magic, a tower for observing the stars, or at least two fine wings added to the massive, obsolete shape of the old house; but this was not in the fellow's habits.

And yet nothing of the kind had been built, neither tower, nor wings, nor keep, not the smallest building was visible. Except that gradually all the building materials seemed to have disappeared and, one fine day, the German workers had left as secretly as they had come, no doubt to return to the heart of their detestable country: I mean the margraviate of Anspach.

What witches' work had these stalwart Teutons carried out? In the devil's name how had they managed to use up so much time and material? People had tried to find out by spying over the outer walls but had not been able to see anything. They had tried to ask the workers a few questions when the latter ventured out into the village; but these savages from Germany did not speak a word of French and nobody in Arcueil knew the infernal patois of Luther. So, they had to rely on conjecture, and, by way of compensation, they did not hold back. Master Jean was capricious, even strange, but his crazy brain and delirious mind could not have given birth to all the ridiculous projects people generously attributed to him.

Henceforth the self-imprisonment of Master Jean d'Anspach became even more strict and complete. From now on the door only opened from time to time to his young nephew who enjoyed the amusement he got from his uncle too much to stop visiting him.

The other would certainly not have weakened his orders towards this demon he feared if he had not thought the young man capable, if necessary, under the pretext of not being able to resist the ardent affection that brought him, of breaking down the door or climbing over the walls. And then, after all, since the young man sometimes carried out the task of bringing him from town the small things he needed, and which he meticulously forgot to pay for, he would grin and bear it, contenting himself with keeping a continuous eye on the youngster, not offering him any sort of meal and triple-locking him in a barn whenever, by chance, he asked to spend the night at the castle.

Master Jean d'Anspach's property comprised at least six walled-in acres of which only two were wooded. To cultivate such an area and keep it in good order many hands would have been needed, a head gardener and several assistants; but our Bavarian was too afraid of anything to do with the human race to allow, on any pretext, a stranger to set foot in the house or to come and share his inhospitable roof. Just as he had never allowed a colleague or apprentice to work in his forge, he never wanted to be helped in his garden; with the result that flower beds, kitchen garden, orchard, meadow and parkland became nothing more than an impenetrable mess, apart from a few spots where Master Jean sowed a little grain and some vegetables.

However, the slender produce of this labour, together with what nature spontaneously gave him, was enough for him to sustain his existence, and especially to keep his safe full. Since he had lived there in seclusion, he had not spent a single gold crown on his subsistence. In summer he ate the roots he dug up from the soil, the fruit from the trees, the milk from a few goats that roamed on the fallow land; in winter he ate the vegetables and fruit he had stored; but never did a mouthful of bread approach his lips. He would crush his wheat between two stones and the resultant flour allowed him to make a sort of broth that would certainly not have aroused envy amongst the Spartans.[1]

He had also reduced his apparel to the bare necessities. Leather straps or wooden clogs

---

1 The description of this frugal diet may be based on the time around 1833 that Borel had spent, after the financial failure of the publication of *Champavert*, in Le Baizil, in Champagne, living in a wooden shack and cultivating the little strip of land in front of it.

on his feet, a woollen blanket in the centre of which he had made a hole for his head, in the manner of certain American Indians, and which he fastened around his body with a length of rope, these just about composed the whole of his outfit. And certainly, it would have been a strange and frightful sight for someone caught unawares, the image of this old man dressed in rags, reduced to the state of a skeleton, dragging himself through the scrubland and stubble, or squatting and huddled, on cold days moving from place to place to follow the oblique rays of a lukewarm sun, like a wild animal frozen stiff by the cold, like a beggar trying to revive his exhausted and sick limbs.

Making use of the privilege given by his holy character, the curate of Arcueil, a good and worthy priest, was the only person to exchange from time to time a few words with our hermit, to beard the lion in his den. During his walks when he was passing by the door he would knock boldly until the other would come, not to open the door, but to place his glistening, watery eye at the small spyhole. And then, in the friendly form of a joke, he would give him good advice suitably packaged, in a vague and roundabout way, little admonitions which might have given Master Jean d'Anspach much to ponder on insofar as he still retained a scrap of his original soul.

One day the priest said to him: "The charity and care of the pastor must extend to the whole flock. His love is for the sick sheep and for the sheep that has gone astray. Permit me Sir, even though unfortunately I know that you are a Protestant, to ask you quickly if you are alive or dead, and whether you need anything for your body or soul, even in the solitude in which you live?"

Whereupon Master Jean sent the good priest away without listening to him and abruptly closed his window.

On another occasion M. le Curé, having had the little spyhole opened again, contented himself with gently letting drop the following phrase: "*Rare solus*", no doubt alluding to one of Saint Augustine's aphorisms.[1] To this the old lynx replied maliciously, and quoting the same text, seeing that the good priest was accompanied by his housekeeper: "*Nunquam duo*".[2]

On another day the priest said to him; "Whether your harvest, in the fruitful days of summer, has been abundant or mediocre,

---

1 Probably the aphorism translated into English as "God loves each of us as if there were only one of us".
2 "Never two".

remember that your harvest comes from God. Divide it into ten shares; but ensure that He who has given you the nine others should at least have the tenth for Himself."

"The tithe, Sir," replied the old goldsmith, "is an odious tax imposed on someone who works by someone who plants no seeds. There is no point in insisting, Sir, I will not give a penny."

"The word of God, my Protestant friend," continued the noble pastor, "is no less precious than a seed of wheat or of rye, and the person who scatters it in the furrows of the soul may be regarded as a farm labourer. Besides the tithe, Sir, is the most equitable tax; it takes from those who have and is not imposed on those who have not."

Sometimes in winter the holy rector would also tell him: "I have poor souls who are suffering and who are cold; what can you do to help us console them and give them warmth?"

But the man whose heart had been dried up by avarice would reply: "Can't you see that I am poor too, and that I live away from people and in the deepest penury?"

Thus, he always made a display of putting forward his hideous parody of poverty in order to mask his true condition and to make his wealth more secure.

IX

FOR several years Master Jean d'Anspach had been living his life like this as a hermit when suddenly he disappeared from his retreat and from the world noiselessly, silently, murkily, vaguely just as in other times it was considered good taste for great legislators to disappear as soon as their laws had been promulgated.

It was again our good and vigilant curate who was the first to draw attention to this absence.

Having knocked several times at the door of the Lutheran without getting a reply, he naturally suspected that the old man might be dead or dying in some nook of his dwelling, needing either medical care or burial.

Straightaway, at his behest, the doors had been broken down and the crowd, always on the lookout for excitement, had rushed from all over into the hated and until now impenetrable hideout of the miser.

One person believed he had heard the old heretic weeping at the bottom of the well, another thought he heard him crying out in the bushes or the cellars. But I leave you to imagine how great must have been the astonishment of the local notables and of the crowd who had hurried to be present at the opening of the house when, after a widespread hunt and a most detailed search, no trace or vestige of Master Jean had been found that could give any indication as to his fate.

Just as big a surprise was the state of abandonment both inside and outside the house. Everywhere there was the most complete starkness: no furniture, no clothes, no utensils, no tools, nothing to recall that a being created in the image of God and of men, belonging to a formerly civilised race, had spent several years of his life there. As it was known that he had neither annuities nor assets in land, the popular idea was that Master Jean's wealth must be wholly metallic. As a result, they had expected to walk on gems and silverware, to find heaps of gold in each room, and everywhere chests full to the brim with silver coins. But, apart from a few musty old coins found at the bottom of a purse, not a single posthumous crown was found at the house of our rich fellow, not even enough to place an honest stake in a game of pharaoh or basset.[1]

Then they remembered the time when the German workers stayed in the house, the considerable quantity of materials that had been brought in at that time, and which these foreigners must have used on some hidden buildings, and they started to search for this construction.

At the entrance to the grounds there was quite a vast cavern, I can't say whether it was natural or artificial, of the type that sometimes are built in magnificent gardens. It was here especially that the most detailed searches were carried out.

Convinced that it was through this grotto that one would reach an underground apartment, several feet of soil were dug up all around; the roof was probed, holes were made in the walls, several enormous stones were moved, but nothing came of these new attempts. No orifice opened, no large rock suddenly swung open on magic hinges, no cavity resounded to the pickaxes of the workers.

---

1 Old French card games.

At this juncture the district Provost had brought in his policemen and had sought the nephew of Master Jean d'Anspach in Paris, hoping to obtain through this intermediary some information about the disappearance of his uncle, or at least a few hints of greater certainty that could surely guide him.

However, at the *Croix de Lorraine*[1] where the young man had lived since his arrival in Paris, they were very anxious about him; he had not been seen for about three weeks.

This was scarcely helpful in shedding light on the matter.

After an arrest warrant for the young foreigner, and a few pursuits that equally had no positive result, justice withdrew its flame with which vainly it had tried to illuminate the darkness. Everyone quickly agreed to resign themselves to knowing nothing.

However, the coincidence of the disappearance of the nephew and the uncle did not put an end to the deductions and conjectures; they simply added to the source of the guesswork. It was generally agreed that the young man had fled to Germany, having stolen the riches of his uncle and that, during one of his last visits,

---

1 Cross of Lorraine.

he had no doubt killed him and buried him in some remote spot in the garden.

As for us, fine people that we are, let us not rush to any conclusions but continue the story.

Following these events, since there was nobody to inherit the castle of Master Jean d'Anspach, it was sold with the profits going to the state as was the custom at the time.

From the hands of the first purchaser, it passed successively into the hands of several others, during the last century, and the old German hoarder and the burial of his loot were quickly forgotten by the new owners and lords of the manor.

But cottage-dwellers have a better memory and the hyperbolic wealth and extraordinary life of Master Jean the Miser had made such an impact on the minds of the villagers that they left deeper traces. This led to the tradition that the local peasants and working people in Paris continued to designate the cavern in the grounds as the hiding place of an immense treasure hidden there in the past by a sort of German Jew,[1] a goldsmith and moneylender to the King, who was so rich, so rich, it was said, that he could have filled a well with his gold.

1 Note the trope in the popular mind that Master Jean must be a Jew because of his profession. He was as we have seen earlier a Lutheran.

In more recent times, when occult procedures, the seekers of spirits and the seekers of underground riches became as it were fashionable, it was especially towards the region of Arcueil that, because of its notoriety, were directed all looks, all hopes, all explorations.

X

A T the end of this story and explana-
tions M. de Brederode would say to his
companions:

"There you have it, gentlemen, the story of
the treasure hidden in the cavern at Arcueil, as
I had heard it from the good prior and his disciples, people with whom a very regrettable fate
had made me get involved, and moreover such
as I remember having read a few years ago, when
I was still at liberty, in a notebook handwritten,
it is said, by M. de l'Estoile[1] himself, which had
been found among other papers at the castle of
Sully-sur-Loire. I don't think, he would add, that
I have forgotten or altered any important detail,
for I would be really surprised because what I
have learned, even only in passing, normally
fixes itself perfectly in my memory."

---

1 Pierre de l'Estoile (1546-1611) was a diarist.

At this point our prisoner's audience, who had listened attentively to the tale we have just heard, would gracefully thank him for the excellent story about Master Jean d'Anspach, and beg him, if it were not asking too much of his good will, to continue with the tale of his own misfortunes which not only aroused the interest of the heart but had the gift of charming the mind.

How could one resist such politeness especially when one is longing to give in? M. de Brederode, in that agreeable embarrassment of the orator applauded by the crowd, would happily accede and then briskly reply: "You wish it, I shall obey; I shall pick up again the thread of the story which involves me more personally, or at least more particularly the crowd of necromancers I was following in my amateurish way."

XI

O N the day fixed by the devil, or rather by his accomplice the monk, for the definitive delivery of the treasure, in other words, as we have stated earlier, the new moon, all our visionaries were faithfully at the meeting place with that laudable punctuality characteristic of people who have invested in a business and who have no desire to see their mountain give birth to a mouse.

This time the plan had been totally changed. It was no longer at the inn on the Place de Grève that our gathering had happened but at midnight, outside the city walls, at the Porte Gibard or d'Enfer,[1] in the abandoned yard of a former tile factory, and with empty stomachs.

With empty stomachs! Yes, empty stomachs! This is what our reverend mystagogue

_____
1 Sometimes also called the Porte Saint-Michel.

had wanted, putting down to our turbulence and to our inebriation the lack of success of our previous attempts. As far as I was concerned, in my role of non-believer and simple visiting brother, thinking that it was sufficient to follow the Ten Commandments of the church and to keep vigil for Saint Andrew and Saint John, I had secretly lined my stomach with a flagon of Burgundy, a good dish of beans and a hearty portion of lamb.

As we made our way, after many preparatory speeches, exhortations and admonitions from the venerable prior, who seemed to be renewing the miracle of the multiplication, not of loaves and fishes, but of words, we arrived at the mound of our sorceress. Everything in the surrounding area was calm and peaceful. We heard neither the horrible barking of the companions of Ulysses who had been changed into wolves and were rattling their chains in the holy wood, nor rustling, nor terror. The whole of nature seemed to be paying the same attention to our stealthy and winding progress as does an entomologist observing the peregrinations of a few insects.

The lapis-lazuli sky speckled and spotted with stars from the zenith to the horizon, with the white sash of the milky way on top, was creating a frieze and backdrop of the greatest splendour. Large groups of dark, strangely shaped trees, through which we were sometimes walking, created the effect of natural and well-defined theatrical wings; the unseen nightingale was singing. It is certain that never has a human action, tragic or holy, had a more magnificent theatre, a more grandiose stage. But God said to the serpent: on thy belly shalt thou go; to man: thou shalt labour; to the ridiculous: thou shalt mingle with the sublime;— that is the law.

What indeed were we? A few idlers, a few dupes grotesquely on our way to ask the bosom of the earth for the payment of a sum it did not owe us: the bosom of the earth, this eternal and disapproving sanctuary, abyss of discretion and of silence, the betrayal of a secret! We might just as well have asked Master Jean d'Anspach to untie his purse strings.

At two in the morning, we were finally arranged in front of the entrance to the cavern, all with one knee on the ground, whilst our Prior, prostrate, kept repeating these three words to which he no doubt gave a sacramental meaning: *Rorate coeli desuper.*[1]

---

1 "Drop down, ye heavens". The opening words of Isaiah 45.8. Part of the Christian liturgy during Advent.

Suzanne, standing in the middle of the group, in a sort of ecstatic state, looked like Judith[1] singing on the mountain the canticle of the action of graces.

She was uniquely beautiful, this young soothsayer, with her generous and picturesque figure, her bright eyes, her pale complexion, the forest of her hair wound gracefully and negligently around her head like a turban and embellished with gold sequins in her plaits.

It is true that whatever variety of dress she wore suited her perfectly, this daughter of Eve. As we have said before, she was charming whatever she wore; however, I could not stop my heart proclaiming that on this night she surpassed herself. She looked like one of those great creatures of the ancient races of the world, a courtesan from Babylon or Tyre, a prophetess of Hermopolis or of Jepher.

A fine silk jerkin or farthingale with broad orange and amethyst stripes, creating an interplay of lines and meeting like an arrowhead on the seams, tightly enclosed the outlines of her waist like damask stretched over the delicate shaft of a column. From this tight, figure-hugging bodice, decorated with gold braid,

1 A widow who murdered a sleeping Holofernes in his tent, cut off his head and returned with it to Bethulia.

there spread in large layers, like the water in a fountain, a moire skirt undulated in the moon's reflection and was long enough to bathe and mysteriously veil her feet, so pretty in their oriental sandals.

Below her beautiful neck, which swayed like a graceful reed, there were wrapped several strands of a necklace of large pearls; these brilliant pearls seemed to embed themselves in the porphyry of her shoulders like the ring of rich fusaroles that encloses in its elegant circle the campana and the acanthus leaves of a Corinthian column capital.

In her hands, as small as lilies, as white as the calyx of an azalea, she was holding a divining rod that she was casually bending like a hunting bow. Oh Suzanne, did ever Amazon, did ever Penthesilia[1] herself more elegantly crack her whip on the flank of her steed? Did ever a queen, black or white, from Ethiopia or Thule, clutch her sceptre more seductively?

But what am I saying? Sceptres or kingdoms of sovereigns, you are no more than vanity and misery. There is but one single sceptre and one single law, and that is the sceptre and law of beauty!

----

1 An Amazonian queen.

This was the speech to Madame de Cythère[1] that I was enthusiastically composing whilst our fat prior, in his clumsy and heavy way, continued to address Latin prayers to I know not which genie of heaven or hell, and whilst his followers were languishing in the humblest piety at the feet of Suzanne.

I don't know why I was so aroused, but at that moment I was in a very unusual state of exaltation. I would willingly have started to act out the story of the three thieves and the donkey,[2] renewed the rape of Helen[3] and abandoned then and there, in their more or less downcast state, this whole band of poor souls lacking either wit or florins.

In this wonderful excitement, with my gaze fixed on Suzanne's pink lips, I was telling myself that nothing transmutes our inner being better than the flame of admiration, for nothing at-

---

1 Madame de Cythère was also the name of the Countess du Barry (1743-1793), the last official mistress of Louis XV. But this would be an anachronism in Brederode's account. It may just be a reference to Venus as the Greek island of Cythera was also supposed to be the birthplace of the goddess Venus.

2 A reference to a fable of Jean de la Fontaine, in which, whilst three thieves are busy arguing about stealing a donkey, a fourth makes off with the beast.

3 Paris, a Trojan prince, seduced Helen, the wife of King Menelaus of Sparta, thereby starting the Trojan war.

tracts more quickly to the shepherd's crook and to the sheep pen—If I were that agile wasp in my striped, mobile bodice I would go and hang my alveola on this coral mouth! If I were the joyous little wren looking for man's dwelling place, I would build my nest of fragrant grass in the thick plaits of her long hair!—But suddenly I noticed a reaction of surprise amongst all of those involved in our adventure and I thought I heard the prior call out in terror: "We are surrounded!"

I turned round and in fact I saw that we were surrounded, not this time in a magic circle, but in a large cordon of foot soldiers, their muskets on their shoulders and their sabres drawn.

I must admit that this did rather cut short my poetic thoughts and I began to curse like a soldier in the Swiss Guard, without being able to manage the transition more skilfully.

However, the manoeuvre had been skilfully carried out. One must be able quickly to recognise real merit when you meet it; and certainly, the Abbé de Pure[1] never had the pleasure of seeing a *coup de théâtre* more subtly executed in the famous *salle des machines*.[2]

---

1 Michel de Pure (1620-1680) was a treasurer and councillor to Louis XIV.
2 An auditorium in the Théâtre des Tuileries in Paris that was noted for its technical effects.

Bravo, I said to the Prior, that's a fine ambush! What do you think, Father? Personally, I find the move deliciously well played!

The poor man was in a terrible trance. With a changed expression and trembling like a leaf he replied sadly, no doubt wishing to allude to the treachery of the apostle Judas: One of us, Sir, will buy the potter's field.[1]

At this moment the ranks of the armed men surrounding us opened and moved apart respectfully to allow through a few unprepossessing armed servants and also a figure walking in front, dressed in a rich gown and bearing a ceremonial sword. This man had the appearance of a very gallant knight.

"In the name of the King, gentlemen," he said removing his large hat decorated with feathers, "I arrest you."

It was the Lieutenant-General of police, Count Voyer d'Argenson;[2] several of us recognised him straightaway but this only made us more concerned and silent. He continued:

"How can it be, gentlemen, that despite all the displeasure the King has shown about all

1 The field said to have been bought by Judas Iscariot using the thirty pieces of silver earned by betraying Christ.
2 D'Argenson became Lieutenant-General of police in 1697 and held the post for 21 years. He was a close confident of Louis XIV.

occult and demonic practices and operations; notwithstanding his injunctions, commands and interdictions, and the order given again and again to all the parliaments and the chamber of justice of the Arsenal to track down and severely punish all the troublemakers with their claimed sorcery, that you come and come again, imprudently to commit the most harmful and guilty acts? Really, that is not good!"

Then turning to each one of us, he addressed us individually, with confidence, using all our names and titles, as if we were old acquaintances. The police are marvellous in this respect. Not a living soul escapes their spies. Everything is recorded, I believe, in their registers as in the book of destiny. Turning first to our monk who seemed the most fearful and had the most astonished expression on his face:

"You, especially, the Prior of Bacheville, you will allow me," he said gently and politely, "to let you know personally how disappointed I am. It upsets me that, despite your holy character, you, a man of religion and of the church, who ought to be a true light and an example to all, you should be the first person to be placing a stumbling-block in front of the footsteps of the blind man. Too bad, the King is really in a rage with you!"

Turning next to Father Le Bègue, organist to the King and to the royal parish of Saint-Roch, he went on:

"You will agree at least, you, M. Le Bègue, whose good attitude and talent I have no hesitation in honouring, that the King is often badly served by his officers, even by those on whom he has bestowed the greatest favours. Believe me, the art in your hands is worth far more than the science of alchemy."

Next came the turn of the old Chevalier Bois-du-Val, of a certain Hans Wilhem Boscus, canon of the Bishop of Munster, of a rich apothecary from Hurepoix, of an actor in Molière's troupe and of a few others besides, who received in turn a smart blow on the knuckles. The Lieutenant-General was so well informed about all our companions that he went from one to another in our groups, speaking directly to the accused in a formal manner.

However, thanks to my privileged status, I was hoping to escape this awkward review, and to do so I was hiding as best I could behind the shoulders of our huge canon from the Palatinate when M. d'Argenson, approaching me and bowing with a demeanour that was more severe than flattering, which I could well have done without, said to me loudly:

"I would have been surprised, Monsieur de Brederode, if the Low Countries had not been represented in this business since they never miss providing their contingent to everything the King finds disagreeable."

"I am here, Monseigneur, neither as the representative of my nation, nor as the representative of my personal tastes," I replied quickly. "All you see in me is a dilletante, a follower, an amateur."

But, no doubt, he did not take in what I had said. He had just been struck, dazzled, by the appearance of Suzanne who was coming out of the cavern into which, when the soldiers arrived, she had hastily retreated.

Heavens above, it was enough to turn the heads of every magistrate in France! . . . The poor child's confusion, her commotion these only added to the natural prestige of her charms. She decidedly had the inspired look and the majestic appearance of a Sibyl.

On my word as a gentleman, Virgil himself would have thought she was Dido and M. l'abbé de Fénelon that she was Calypso![1]

You should have seen the Lieutenant-General, with an arrow in his heart, tilt his head then immediately step back to make the

---

1 A reference to a novel by François Fénelon in 1699 *The adventures of Telemachus.*

famous bow in three stages of the bourgeois gentleman, whilst trying, like an old cat, to hide its claws in the velvet.

He said to her:

"I have heard about you in the most flattering terms, Mademoiselle de la Filandière" (it appears that was Suzanne's name; as I have already remarked the police know everything); "but truth surpasses expectation. You are from Bordeaux, are you not, or at least from Les Landes near Bordeaux? The women from your region are exceptionally beautiful! . . . I regret that with so many eminent qualities to arouse an honourable interest in your favour you were indulging in regrettable actions, in the endeavours of a charlatan. But you are young, and we have saved some who have spent more years in hell than you."

"I don't know, Sir," replied Suzanne, "that it can be so bad to reclaim from the earth goods that have been entrusted to it either through fear or folly, and that could be enormously helpful for the living."—Then she added with a grin:—"If the King finds that reprehensible, it must be that he is bored with Madame de Maintenon,[1] and that he must be in a bad mood."

---

1 Madame de Maintenon (1635-1719) was the secret wife of Louis XIV, although she was never considered to be Queen of France.

To begin with Monsieur d'Argenson seemed quite surprised by this rather outrageous theory. However, he received the quip courteously, contenting himself with placing two fingers on the ravishing lips of the beautiful necromancer, to indicate to her that, even if one were a pretty girl, one should speak with more respect about the King.

It transpired, that the previous visits we had made to Arcueil and of which we thought people were unaware had been perfectly well-known, just like everything that we think is highly secret. The rumour had spread in the city. The weekly broadsheet had mentioned our visits. In it the editor wrote about our prior in very unflattering terms. He suggested, and this is something I shall always find hard to believe, that the prior was getting money from rich and credulous people, with the pretext of getting them to subsidise the material expenses of the operations and to involve them in the future profits. If this were true, I had no chance to check it for myself. The chap took me to be a drain on resources; besides I was a neophyte of too tardy and too tottering faith. I have always paid little attention to these remarks. I know that these newspapers live only through treachery and sarcastic articles. They would find poison in the pink beak of a dove.

The King had read the article. The whole court had talked about it one evening when there was a reception, especially Monsieur de Beauvilliers, Monsieur de Cavoye et Monsieur du Maine, and straightaway a clear order had been given to the Lieutenant-General that he should bring the scandal to an end immediately.—Thus, there was no unfaithful apostle, no traitor, no false brothers, as our prior was disposed to believe. That's how we are, we prefer to pick on the well-known wickedness of man than on the natural run of events.

XII

WHILST COUNT D'ARGENSON, full of admiration for Suzanne, had been putting on airs and graces, he had surreptitiously made a secret gesture to the scowling men around him; and they, pushing immediately on the springs of little shaded lanterns hidden under their cloaks and which suddenly spread a bright light around them, had gone into the cavern stealthily. It seems as though this was what the Lieutenant-General's sign had invited them to do.

After a thorough search, like true police bloodhounds, they soon came out triumphantly, carrying very many objects that they laid at the feet of the Lieutenant-General: optical and fantasy-world instruments, hazel-nut branches, torches, parchments, megaphones. In their midst was a man struggling like a demon and whose costume recalled that worn by the devil in a play. A black mask covered his face and he had two false horns on his forehead.

At this sight my companions were overcome with terror; I, however, was delighted to see the devil between two police officers, and I was overjoyed that, for once in his life, he who likes playing bad tricks on us should find himself in serious difficulty.

But the Lieutenant-General, who was strong-minded and doubtless had little faith in the existence of underground genies, did not allow me to enjoy this gentle satisfaction for long; he cheerfully walked up to the phantom and with a bold and profane gesture he ripped off his horns and his mask.

Imagine our excitement when, stripped of his insignia, we recognised that this prince of darkness was none other than François, our reverend prior's servant!

I confess that, just for a moment, this masquerade with all the optical and catoptrical instruments, lanterns, mirrors and many other objects of more or less unknown use made me agree with the views of the journalist of whom we have recently spoken and who insidiously hinted in his newspaper that the good monk, the initiator of our project, was tricking his followers. But I quickly chased away this evil thought; I blushed that with such an unjust suspicion I could in my mind have tarnished the purity of intention of such an honest man. But there we have it! Our soul can not be responsible for the bad thoughts that surprise and pass through it. It has no more capacity than has the lily to close its calyx, no matter how white and pure, at the approach of hornets or wasps, and bad thoughts are the hornets of our soul.

Suddenly piercing cries were heard from the direction of the parkland. That was all we needed to cause us to swoon. We were passing from one fainting fit to another, from surprise to surprise. It was enough to drive you mad, to lose your head, in this conflict of catastrophes. However, M. d'Argenson, who was always in control whichever way the wind blew, did not bother himself with such a trifle.

With his normal calm and phlegm, as if he had his ears blocked up, he commanded his archers to gather up the evidence and to take us to a place of safety in an apartment in the castle, where we would remain under close guard. Then he specifically ordered that Mlle Suzanne be put in a suitable drawing room on her own, and that they should pay her the greatest respects. Clearly, the lyre of Orpheus had moved the stone which seems to replace the heart in a magistrate.

This delicate gesture did not satisfy the Lieutenant-General's need to be amorous and tender.

"I will be with you shortly, mademoiselle; go without fear," he said to her, touching her hand affectionately.

XIII

WHILST we were taken, two by two, to our provisional prison, M. d'Argenson and a few of his close colleagues headed towards the part of the park where the noise was coming from, guided by the cries that were echoing even more piercingly.

They plunged into a sort of impassable avenue blocked by stalks and branches and reached, through intertwined boughs and tortuous and broken-off roots, a clump of trees and shrubs as dense and compact as the mesh of a bower. In the midst of this protection there was a small spot covered only by tall tufty grass and a few climbing plants, some hops and ivy. Beneath this grass they noticed a small amount of freshly moved earth and a hole that looked as though it had been recently formed by a landslide. It was from the depths of this hole that were escaping, just as the sulphur and fiery larva shoots up from the depths of Vesuvius, the cries that were filling with their tumult the profound calm of the night and of the woods.

"Good Lord!" said M. d'Argenson, "there's someone here who, for God's sake, has not taken a vow of silence with the Abbé de Rancé!"[1]

"That's true, Count, and who, moreover, did not find peace in the bosom of the earth, that asylum of rest," added one of the servants of the Lieutenant-General, leaning over the precipice and plunging his lantern into the opening.

By the lamplight it was easy to pick out beneath the disturbed earth stone steps going downwards similar to the stairs that give access to cellars in our houses.

"Whether it be the ladder leading to the devil's mill or some other snare leading to some other bad place, bah! I am going to risk it," said the same policeman.

And as best he could he began to slide into the crater and courageously to descend into the ravine.

"Go on, go on, I am following you," said M. d'Argenson; "but let's take care not to renew the rather dated story of Empedocles."[2]

---

1 L'Abbé de Rancé (1626-1700) the founder of the Trappist order. Trappist monks are supposed to speak only when necessary and to avoid idle talk.

2 The Greek philosopher Empedocles is supposed to

Having groped their way very carefully down about twenty steps covered with the earth that had collapsed, they found themselves on a landing or rather the floor of a small underground chamber, in the middle of which was an enormous, blackened object which, shouting and groaning, was thrashing about and making useless efforts to get up like a cockchafer put on his back by a schoolboy.

Our bold adventurers approached this shapeless and sinister mass with redoubled caution as in olden times the Trojans approached the infamous horse. They first explored the most extreme parts and discovered, to begin with, a hand and a shoe, then a knee and an elbow, then the other leg and the other arm, all of them joined to a gigantic abdomen, which ended with a fat human face disfigured by a hideous expression: it was the fat face of our reverend prior.

Count d'Argenson recognised him immediately but rather by his corpulence than his features.

"What the devil are you doing here, Monsieur de Bacheville, and in such a state?" he said to him in a friendly way.

"Alas, Lieutenant, I almost broke my bones and lost my life! I don't know where I am; all I

---

have thrown himself into the crater of Mount Etna.

know is that the earth gave way under me and that I rolled for a long time like a tennis ball in a *jeu de paume*.[1]

"No harm done. That'll be nothing, reverend. Come along, my friends, put the gentleman back on his feet.

"Easier said than done," retorted the agent who had been the first to set foot in the abyss, biting his lip so as not to laugh.

Then four of the most robust police officers grabbed hold of our saintly man, and, hauling him up as a jack raises a burden, they put him back on his feet as best they could.

After this enterprise had been carried out, these fine men could have said, following the example of Horace: *Exegimus monumentum*;[2] but they contented themselves, on the orders of the Lieutenant-General, to drag the poor monk from this unpleasant receptacle and to bring him to the castle to be with his disciples, that's to say us, in the apartment where we were locked up.

Once we were over our initial terror it did not take us long to notice that the prior was not present in our prison. After the defeat, in

---

1 A game that is a forerunner of lawn tennis, still played with the name of 'real tennis', derived from 'royal tennis'.
2 A misquotation of Horace but the meaning is "we demand a monument".

the prisoner of war camp where the enemy has taken them, the first task of the vanquished is to call the roll and to count how many are there. When the wolf is on the prowl, the pastor also counts his sheep; but here the sheep were reduced to counting themselves since the leader of the herd was missing. The good monk was the very soul of the enterprise and the soul of the majority of those carrying it out. Thus, once this absence was noticed, it only spread new alarms and added to the discouragement in the company.

How could it be that he was not with us? In his role as leader of the choir, had he been obliged to bear the whole weight of the Lieutenant-General's anger? Out of respect for his character and his rank, had he carefully been separated from us, in the same way as Suzanne had been because of her sex and her beauty? To each according to his whim a more or less bizarre, more or less plausible explanation for this disappearance. Those who were devoted to the prior with sincere faith, and who revered him and occult science with exaggerated zeal, only wished to see in this absence the result of a faculty common to all true believers, that of vanishing into the darkness. From impossibility to impossibility these fervent disciples had arrived at the most miraculous outcomes in honour of their master. Already a few of them were talking vaguely of apotheosis, of transfiguration. They had seen him suddenly, in the midst of the general hubbub, or at least they thought they had seen him, if they were not the plaything of some illusion, gently leave the earth, fade, get smaller, become pure spirit and rise up to the heavens.

Things had reached this degree of exaltation and it was generally agreed that our reverend prior, reduced to the state of a totally metaphysical being, was walking amongst the stars to evade the lawsuits of the Lieutenant-General of Police, when, unfortunately, this admirable metamorphosis, which so ingeniously recalled the transformation of Daphne,[1] or the transubstantiation of Chapelain's wig,[2] received a severe denial.

The door of the apartment where we were imprisoned had suddenly been opened, and the weighty mass of M. de Bacheville, more terrestrial and more material than ever, had been pushed into our midst by the four police

---

1 The goddess Daphne had herself transformed into a laurel tree to escape the amorous advances of Apollo.
2 Jean Chapelain (1595-1674) was a poet. In a comic poem Boileau (1636-1711) has Chapelain's wig transformed into a comet.

officers who had just carried out the extraction of the poor astrologist.

Upon this so perfectly unannounced reappearance, the surprise, as can easily be imagined, was widespread; but the accompanying prestige, I must admit, had a rather mediocre effect. To the disorder of his expression and his speech, the unfortunate prior joined the disorder of his dress; and our enlightened colleagues had to change their minds when the fellow, pressed by their questions, got to tell them how, escaping from the crowd and seeking a hiding place in the park, he had prosaically fallen into a hole.

But whilst the good M. de Bacheville was regaling us in detail with the tiniest aspects of his accident (which came incidentally to cheer me up for I was being badly overcome with melancholy and beginning to bitterly regret having joined in the stupidity of these insignificant folk), the Lieutenant-General of Police was pursuing his investigations in the vault in the park.

So, let us leave our brave monk to tell, retell and retell again in the tiniest details the story and the infrequent and unvaried episodes of his fall, which we can flatter ourselves that we already know in sufficient detail.

XIV

WHEN, as we have just seen, Count d'Argenson had got rid of the prior, and now that he was the serene master of the place, he began to examine carefully where he was. It was a sort of small chamber measuring about twelve feet at most in all directions, built from very spotless stone that had been very skilfully assembled. The floor was covered with large, beautiful tiles of beige limestone. There was a low frieze around the walls, and a surbased barrel vaulting, built in the German style by a very skilful craftsman, was supported on an architrave of quite simple design but of good taste.

M. d'Argenson was beginning to wonder what the origin of this underground building was and what could be its possible use. And because he was, so it seems, a believer in that school of history which holds, and I have not the slightest notion why, that the goddess Isis had formerly left her beautiful country in the East to come and be worshipped in the sub- urbs of Lutetia,[1] he was trying to discover in this totally recent and modern masonry some ancient substructure, a few vestiges of a temple formerly built on this spot, in honour of the afore-mentioned goddess, when suddenly he spotted at floor level, and aligned with the flag- stones, in an angle of the vault, on the opposite side to the steps where our dear prior had made such a perilous descent, an opening or orifice similar to the mouth of a well and of about the same diameter.

Great was his surprise, his archaeological surprise I mean, and moving on to new con- clusions he began to investigate this continuing similarity in the floor, and what could be the purpose and the meaning.

Then he saw below him, in the depths of this sort of cylinder, a flight of stone stairs at- tached to a common central post and forming what is commonly called a spiral staircase, an Archimedes screw, as can be found in old Gothic buildings, inside belfries and clock towers.

---

1 The Roman city of Lutetia was the predecessor of Paris. It was believed that Isis came to Gaul with the Romans.

The Lieutenant-General's servant who, lantern in hand, had been the first to risk entering this den by the perilous route so picturesquely taken by M. de Bacheville, this servant, say I, was the first who dared go into this new narrow space, so tight that a man could scarcely pass.

M. d'Argenson was not naturally fearful, and with a resolute step he began to go down, step by step, on the heels of his servant. Nothing is more contagious than fear or courage.

After several revolutions that the staircase made around its stone axle, they found themselves at the bottom of the steps, in a vault that was similar to the one they had just explored higher up. Only here the walls were polished like marble, and the stones obliquely cut in the Florentine manner, and arranged with that special art to be seen in the facades of Tuscan palaces.

From the groined vaulted ceiling delicately cut and with veins at the edges, there was suspended an old candelabra. The stones on the surface still bore the traces of the smoke given off by a flickering flame, extinguished now for more than a century, having for too long regretfully illuminated with its confident light the bouts of the most disgusting human passion, the love of gold; having witnessed, as it died itself, a scene of horror and despair.

M. d'Argenson paid scant attention to all this. A narrow passage, open before him, in the thickness of one of the walls of the vault, closed by an iron grill, had attracted the whole of his attention.

Beyond this second room there was thus another chamber into which this passage and this door must lead. And in there, and beyond, what was there? An infinite succession of hideouts leading from one to the other and stretching far into the darkness, like those natural galleries where the lost visitor often meets a solitary and horrible end, would they steal away and flee before their footsteps as far as the abysses of the earth?

He trembled, he hesitated.

Finally, overcoming this first onset of terror that he could not prevent, with the conspicuous bravery so fitting for a magistrate, he drew close to the side where the mysterious exit was built into the side of the wall. This stone bay looked quite like the opening to a huge furnace.

The Lieutenant-General walked to the end of the embrasure that was so tight that he could barely stand up, and when he was face to face with the iron grill that blocked the opening, he tried to push it. But the obstacle did not give way.

Behind the grill the darkness was so profound that the eye could not discern either dimensions or shapes. M. d'Argenson passed the lantern guiding him through two of the bars and moving around this pale and flickering light he gradually began to pick out, in a sort of cell completely built from stone like the previous vaults, a variety of chests and furniture along the walls.

On the floor not far from the grill, two shapeless and blackish lumps were lying not far from one another.—They looked like two dead bodies stretched out on the floor.

Staring for a long time at these bizarre sights whose unclear outlines were blurred by the opaque darkness, in order to try to pick out a less uncertain silhouette, some more precise indication that might help him to unravel the ambiguity of these strange objects, Count d'Argenson ended up recognising, in a way which no longer allowed any doubt, that these were two figures in the immobility of death, two human bodies thrown there on the ground, like skeletons snatched from their coffins and trampled underfoot on a day of anger and profanation.

Just as this certainty promptly and rapidly took hold in his mind, terror slipped into his soul; the cold of fear entered his flesh and froze the blood in his veins. His lantern slipped from his hands, fell on the floor and went out; he walked out backwards, with a strange expression, until he was in the midst of his men who had remained behind him in the vault, as if the two dead bodies had suddenly stood up on their bones and had spoken to him in a sinister voice.

But politeness and elegant customs have no truck with natural manifestations, with naivety of feelings. The Lieutenant-General immediately repressed the involuntary discomfiture that had taken hold of him, discomfiture unworthy of a man of good taste, and so resuming his normal air:—I do not know, he said, whether I have been the dupe of some vision, but I think that I saw in there two sorts of phantoms; yes, two phantoms, two spectres, stretched out on the bottom of that cage, like two turtle doves lying on the sand of a bird cage. "Come here, take a look yourselves, gentlemen, bring a torch!"

The grill was locked with an extremely complicated and very strange mechanism. In vain did they try to find the secret and the combination. Impossible to put the finger on the mysterious spring that would get the door to swing open on its hinges: they had to break the bolt and the latch with an axe.

The practised and penetrating eye of M. d'Argenson had not been mistaken in the darkness; he had picked out perfectly what was contained in the cell. There were indeed, as he had thought, several chests and several barrels which lined the walls, and in addition in the middle of the room two sorts of spectres stretched out on the floor.

One of the two bodies, wrapped in a large woollen mantle tied round him by a rope, looked as though he had been surprised by death in profound poverty. No clothes on his skin, bits of torn leather with holes in them for shoes, held together with remnants of material and string: a hideous imitation of the sandals of a poor mendicant brother.

A forest of long unkempt white hair, and a large white beard which went from his eyes right down to his chest, made an extremely thin face almost invisible. His forehead was wrinkled, his hollow, pale cheeks were criss-crossed by crooked lines; his eye had subsided into its socket and had disappeared beneath the weight of a closed and flattened eyelid; his mouth, still half open, seemed to have been twisted by a last convulsive cry; the whole face had a horrible expression of stupidity and pain. His cruelly emaciated arms, his stiff fists that had been clenched with force, all bore numerous teeth marks; in a few places the flesh was torn and raw as if it had been gnawed with force for a long time. Everything seemed to indicate that this old man must have expired in the most appalling hunger and madness.

The other body was that of a fairly young man. Face down, with his forehead pressed on his crossed hands, he was prostrate at full length, a few feet away from the old man, looking like those large prostrate figures that sculptors sometimes chisel on the lids of tombs to represent the bleak image of despair.

He was dressed from head to foot in crimson, breeches and doublet of a rich and silky material, a sort of velvet. The gown folded over his shoulders was pleasing and elegant but cut in a very old-fashioned style similar to that still seen today worn by certain actors. Around his neck he had a large and beautiful embroidered ruff, and fine lace at his cuffs. In a word, this child, in so far as could be judged from the first investigation of his appearance and the good taste of his clothes, must have been, at the time when he had been so cruelly surprised by death, a very distinguished and fashionable young man.

His face was haggard but white; the beginnings of a blond beard framed his lips and marked out the graceful outline of his chin. His features were delicate and pretty, his hands were small and delicate, and there was on his forehead and the whole of his inanimate and colourless physiognomy an expression of ineffable calm and innocence. It looked as though he had left life without regret, without effort, resignedly. He could not have been more than twenty years old.

We must assume that these underground chambers were of a healthy and salubrious construction, and that the mortal remains of this child and those of the old man had been in a place where there was no ambient damp and no dissolving element, for they were both perfectly preserved, or rather perfectly dried out, as if they had been carefully embalmed in a casket. The dry skin adhering to the joints had taken on the hardness and sonority of parchment, and the flesh and blood had been reduced and vapourised to the point where they were weightless. That is how, so they say, are found in the desert the bodies of travellers swallowed up in sandstorms.

It would not be easy to depict the amazement of the Lieutenant-General of Police and the astonishment of his underlings at such a strange encounter; and what would be especially difficult for me would be to follow them in the host of imagined theories and suppositions set off in their minds by the sight of these two bodies, creating such a curious contrast between them: one very young, the other at the final limit of old age; one showing all the appearances of the most disgusting poverty, the other in the livery of luxury and the finery of elegance; one with a hideous death mask, the image of vice and madness, the other with a fine blond head, resigned and gentle, like that of a sleeping child.

How had these two unfortunates met their death in this dungeon? How long had they been there? Who might they be? Here are just a few of the thousand and one questions that our investigators were naturally asking, as they carried out their sad examination, looking at these poor victims whose end must have been so cruel, and who must have passed away after a slow and awful death agony.

As for us, who are probably better informed than the policemen, it is more than likely that we recognised a long time ago that these two ghosts in the vault were none other than Master Jean d'Anspach and his nephew Adolphus.

XV

IN the short space of time the privileged prisoners had for their recreation, either at the
Bastille or in Vincennes, it was difficult for the
unfortunate M. de Brederode to finish to the
satisfaction of his companions the story of the
misfortunes he claimed to have had, and which
we are trying faithfully to transcribe here. The
importunate appearance of the jailer, who came
to take the prisoners back to their cells, would
interrupt, normally to the great chagrin of the
listeners, the story to which they were listening
and from which they were increasingly taking
an acute and genuine pleasure.

"The next episode tomorrow, gentlemen,"
Count de Brederode would say as he departed:
"Dijon" (for this was the name of the jailer)
"doesn't want you to know any more today."
Then, turning to the key-bearer himself, he

would add: "Dijon, do you know that you are a genuine rhetorical device? You arrive skilfully to frustrate through delay and suspense the flow of my narrative to add to its attractiveness and charm."

And the next day, at the regular time for the walk, when the audience had gathered on the platform, sometimes sitting on an old cannon, which for centuries had aimed its silent mouth towards the city, after a short preamble he would take up the story where he had left it the previous day.

"The eye is rapid," he would normally say, "and speech is slow and sentences, even in the most practised mouth, follow one another slowly like heavily laden carts making way on a narrow, sandy path. Therefore, don't imagine that M. d'Argenson remained for so long next to the two bodies in order to make a close investigation, as I myself did yesterday, so that I could give you only an imperfect, imprecise idea."

At the same time as he was engrossed in this sad assessment and in the feelings which were its natural result, letting his mind sail away on the sea of ideas and hypotheses, M. d'Argenson had slyly and in detail checked all aspects of the cell, to make sure that there was not, as in the preceding vaults, some exit opposite the entry, leading to further underground vaults. But his search could not find a single fissure in the stone, the slightest gap, that might make one suspect that there was a passageway that had been closed off or skilfully hidden; there was no doubt about it, this was the final part of the crypt. However, a new, considerable and extraordinary surprise was still awaiting him.

Suddenly he thought that he saw that one of the barrels in the angle of the wall closest to him, was full, full to the brim, like a packed bushel. He walked over and, under a thick layer of dust, he saw the outline of a large number of small disks similar to coins.—"What can this be?" he wondered. "What funereal money is locked away in these catacombs?

Then, with the sheath of his sword, anxiously and carefully, he touched the objects; he moved a few of them to be certain what he was dealing with: there was a sudden metallic sound; a uniform yellow tint, similar to the colour of gold, offered itself to the reflected light and to his astonished eyes.—There was no doubt, it was gold, gold coins! . . . Gold, this barrel was full of gold, as was that one! . . . One after another five barrels were full of gold guilders and crowns.

M. d'Argenson could not get over his excitement, he went from one to the other, he touched them, he made them chink, he looked at them. "Is this really true?" he cried out; "Is it an enchantment? Am I the object, the victim of some filthy trick played by our magicians, of some witchcraft?"

There were an iron chest and two boxes of sculpted wood in the cell, close to the barrels; their keys were still in their locks. They were soon opened, examined, ransacked; they contained all sorts of ingots, sacks of gold and silver, jewels, precious vases, gems, pearls, precious stones; the richest, the most brilliant, the finest work of a goldsmith. Imagine the treasure of Cleopatra and the treasury of King Louis XI mixed with the riches of Montezuma.

If M. d'Argenson's surprise had been great at the sight of the two spectres stretched out on the floor, it was no less so before this miraculous, incredible, extraordinary discovery. But his delight was greater than his admiration; he thought he was entering the city of the sun and eclipsing for ever the glory of Fernand Cortez and of Pizarro.[1]

This heap of riches alongside the remains of a young man and a hideous old greybeard dressed in rags could scarcely get to the bottom of what was strange and incomprehensible in

1 Two sixteenth-century Spanish conquistadors, Cortez in Mexico and Pizarro in Peru.

all this. It just made the riddle more complicated and the Lieutenant-General's intrigued and astonished mind lost itself again in the depths of suppositions. When our mind is faced with something obscure or of which it is unaware, it rides off into the realms of the imagination.

When M. d'Argenson had well and truly rejoiced, had sated his gaze on all the wonderful things that his good luck had so to speak laid at his feet, amidst the most bizarre circumstances, he finally prepared to leave the cell. First, he ordered his men to leave; but just as he was about to cross the threshold, he thought that he saw something on the ground near the body of the young man.

He retraced his steps and picked up a small lantern, then the remains of a pencil that had been worn down to a stub, and a small pocketbook in embossed leather similar to what today we call a diary or a pocketbook.

M. d'Argenson opened it and glanced quickly at it . . . all the pages were filled with an irregular handwriting, heavily traced with black pencil.

The possession of such an object immediately gave him the hope that he might find some scrap of information, even a whole revelation, a few notes left behind by these victims about the cruel death they had endured underground, and the source of the riches that were hidden there. And so, he took the pocketbook with him.

But since it would not have been prudent to leave the immense treasure in the cell, perfect for putting covetousness into the least greedy of hearts, at the mercy of events and of the first thief who might be tempted to make a visit, he provisionally closed the grill with his cordon of a Knight of the Order of the Holy Spirit,[1] as if to place a royal seal on it and take possession of it in the name of his master, like an explorer who has just set foot on a new land.

Then, with the promise of a significant reward, having ordered his men to maintain a total silence about what they had just seen, he left the vault with them. Then two of the archers were summoned who were keeping us prisoner in the castle and who consequently knew nothing at all about the new discovery; he posted them at the entrance, giving them the formal order to shoot without pity anyone who tried to approach them, with the exception of the Lieutenant-General himself.

---

1 Founded in 1578 by Henri III this was for two and a half centuries the most prestigious of the orders of chivalry in France.

XVI

MORE triumphantly than Jason returning from Colchis having stolen the famous golden fleece, Count Voyer d'Argenson returned to us from his underground expedition.

He came majestically into the apartment where we were incarcerated; his face was bursting with joy and satisfaction; with a smile permanently playing on his lips he begged us not to let ourselves become too bored.

At that moment, as far as I was concerned, I don't think I had an expression of melancholy, for, since the return of our reverend prior, I had been in high spirits and had cracked a large number of jokes about his magic lanterns and about how his valet, M. Jean-François, had been disguised as the devil.

The Lieutenant-General also gave us the consoling thought that our current situation was only provisional, that he was going to write about it to the King of whom he was simply the envoy, and that as soon as His Majesty had communicated his wishes to him, we would no doubt leave this place for a more lasting and more specific location.

Then he left us absorbed in our thoughts, after a few mild jokes about our unfortunate pretension to witchcraft and the infertility of our actions, mischievous remarks the full portent of which we did not understand since we were unaware of the real treasure that M. d'Argenson had encountered, as a result of such a strange adventure, at the bottom of the mysterious den accidentally revealed by the fall of our brave monk and reverend prior.

He immediately went into the salon next door, where Suzanne was imprisoned, and began speedily to prepare his dispatch to the King, for he was longing to inform him of his successes and what he had captured.—For a faithful and zealous servant what agreeable news to bring to his master!

But the indefinable charm of the beautiful sorceress continually attracted his gaze and was unravelling his thoughts and sentences as quickly as they were being assembled and was plunging him into that state of distraction and anxiety felt by unruly schoolboys when they have to do their homework.

As soon as his letter was finished M. d'Argenson put it in an envelope, sealed it and had it taken urgently by a special courier to Marly[1] where the King and his court had been residing for a few days.—It must have been about half past four in the morning.

Free from all urgent cares, under no obligation to activate any of the cogs of his administration, and unable to act until he had the monarch's reply and new orders, the Lieutenant-General saw an agreeable moment of leisure before him.

He drew close to Suzanne, made one or two delicate comments, pronounced one or two honeyed phrases as the Lieutenant-General was so skilled at doing; but the beautiful prisoner did not seem touched at all.

But M. d'Argenson was very keen to begin a conversation with her and said:

"Do you seek treasures, Mademoiselle, everywhere and in no matter what location?"

"We seek them, Sir, wherever they are to be found."

The reply was brief and rather arcane.

---

1 Marly-le-Roi is in the Department of the Yvelines to the west of Paris. The Château de Marly, destroyed in the Revolution, was one of the favourite palaces of Louis XIV.

The Lieutenant-General stopped, somewhat taken aback; then he went on:

"So, you were thinking that there would be a treasure here?"

"Yes, Sir, otherwise we would have looked elsewhere, if not we would have been stupid."

How could you object to such an argument? With difficulty. It was clear, with a strict and narrow logic; it had, as the old hunter's proverb goes, struck the bird in the eye. Therefore M. d'Argenson only tried to use good humour to counter it.

"It's true that you are skilful people," he said mischievously; "but believe me there is a bigger sorcerer than all of us, and this sorcerer is fate."

The Lieutenant-General was smiling secretively, thinking of the instructive fall of the monk.

"But, since you were looking for a treasure," he went on, "even supposing there was one here, where did this belief come from, Mademoiselle?"

The beautiful soothsayer replied:

"You are clearly ill informed, dear Lieutenant-General, for a person with your responsibilities. How are you unaware of something which everyone knows, that is that considerable riches are buried in some part of Arcueil or even somewhere on this property?"

"Really! Who could have hidden these riches? . . . The creator at the beginning of Genesis?"

Like the person who is hiding the cat we are seeking in his sack M. d'Argenson was still playing games.

"No, Sir, it was about a century ago; there was, it was said, an extremely rich miser, goldsmith and money lender to King Henri IV."

At this point Suzanne recounted in a few words what we have known for a long time about Master Jean d'Anspach; and when she had finished her tale, which the Lieutenant-General had listened to, becoming more and more surprised, even amazed, for it all corresponded exactly to what he had seen in the underground room, he said to her half convinced and ready to accept that she was a sorceress, something that he had refused until recently:

"Ah! Who then, Mademoiselle, has managed to remember all this?"

"The common people, Sir, who never forget. Moreover, it must have been set down in a few texts; extremely knowledgeable people have assured me that this is so."

M. d'Argenson allowed himself to spend a few minutes in thought; for this strange affair, this mixture of reality and folly, naturally gave him much to think about. Then he suddenly snapped out of it:

"How clumsy of me, Mademoiselle, to tire you with my questions," he exclaimed, "since I have here a little book that might enlighten me much more? You will allow me, beautiful Circe, won't you? Please believe, Mademoiselle, that I am full of the respects that one should pay to women, and particularly to a woman with your beauty. Ah! Had it not been for an affair of state, I beg you, or rather an affair that concerns the state, you would see me occupied with only you, serving you, trying to delight you! . . . I would remain there at your feet as at the feet of an idol!"

Having started with a delicate madrigal he then finished on the blazing tone of a heroic epistle, that was not too bad, it was even rather good!

And the Lieutenant-General was right to congratulate himself quietly on his worthiness.

XVII

THE writing covering the pages of the small book that M. d'Argenson had found in the stone cell, beside the corpse of the young man, and which to judge by the elegance of its binding, totally in keeping with the elegance of the clothes of this unfortunate man, must certainly have belonged to him, was a fairly legible handwriting but written by a shaky, trembling hand. There was little order in the drafting and no logic in the sequence of pages. The majority of the lines went from down to up or from up to down in a flamboyant way rather like the lines that children are made to draw to initiate them gradually into the mysteries of the upstrokes and downstrokes of handwriting.

On the very first page there was, in quite large letters as though they formed a title:

ADOLPHUS,
NEPHEW OF MASTER JEAN
D'HANSPACH[1]
TO THOSE
WHO MAY ENTER THIS HIDING
PLACE, IF
EVER
HEAVEN PERMITS IT, AND INTO
WHOSE HANDS
THIS LITTLE BOOK SHOULD FALL,
GREETINGS, FRIENDSHIP AND
HAPPINESS.
HAVE PITY ON ME.

This strange beginning, which seemed to promise revelations, was unlikely to dampen down curiosity, quite the opposite. Hooked, intrigued, M. d'Argenson, who was dying to know more, began to decipher the mysterious magic book with the enthusiasm and devotion of a young lady secretly devouring one of those fine novels that transport the soul on a sea of gallantry and love.

Following on from this sort of frontispiece or preface there came this story which may not be absolutely accurate where the language is concerned but is certainly correct when it is a question of the facts.

---

1 Spelt this way in the original text.

The poor, unfortunate nephew of Master Jean d'Anspach began thus:

"My end will no doubt be horrible! I shall expire alongside my uncle in a slow death agony; that is inevitable, inexorable; alongside my uncle on whose brow the cold shadows of death are already falling. And it is to explain my presence in this fateful place, if ever it should be known, and to save my memory from all importunate suppositions or interpretations, that I am taking the trouble to put down in this book the cause and reason for my downfall.—Fate is a really cruel law!

"Everything about my uncle, his trade, his wealth, his riches, his strangeness, his sordidness, sordidness that the poor man, alas, will have expiated so dearly by my mistake: all these details, I say, were only too well known; they had for too long astonished the court and the whole of Paris for it to be necessary for me to dwell on them. Moreover, as I have just written, my only wish, if my lamp whose light is getting dimmer by the minute and my courage do not desert me, is to leave behind a few words of explanation about the horrible event that is taking place at this moment.

"Having left his goldsmithing workshop, or rather his money-lending office, carrying off an immense fortune, my uncle had retired here as everybody knows to Arcueil, to this castle, where he lived in total solitude and in an extraordinary refinement of privations.

"Absolutely nobody came into this retreat, nobody, except me, who would come from time to time to find out how he was and to spend a few hours in his company.

"The aim and the motive of these visits, I hope that people will be fair-minded enough to see, were certainly not based on self-interest. It was neither the welcome nor the excellent meal I would get that could attract me to this lair. What I was doing was also not simply to obey the duty imposed on me by my tutors when they sent me to live in France close to Master Jean, my uncle, not to pass up any means, any hypocrisy, to capture his benevolence, to get him to like me, to charm him, to turn him in my favour, to ensure that I received his gifts (alas, the gifts of my uncle) and the considerable inheritance of which I had a distant hope. No, it was certainly not that, as heaven is my witness, love of money had not yet sullied my heart. I even believe that the state of abjection into which I saw that this passion could plunge a man, had cured me in advance and for ever of the taste for gold, for gold, that vile drug!—

Could a bad example possibly be more effective than a good one?

"If I came to see my uncle it was mainly caused by an honest family feeling. Was he not the brother of my poor mother who I had loved so much? Then there was something in the features of the old man, and sometimes in his voice and his gestures, something that reminded me her; I confess that was enough to make me befriend him.

"But I must also say that there was another more puerile thought in my mind, that will be excused, I hope, because of my extreme youth. My uncle was so bizarre, so strange, so amusing in all his little avaricious practices that each time I was with him I was sure that he would serve me up some new folly and therefore I took a certain secret, sly pleasure in seeing him.

"I had read and reread *The Miser* by Plautus at university. But this miser was no rival for my uncle! How pale and colourless I remembered him! Harpagon,[1] Euclio,[2] Thesaurochrysonicochrysides,[3] compared with my uncle, were profligate."

1 The central character in Molière's *L'Avare* (1668) [Tr. as *The* Miser] based on *Aulularia* by Plautus.
2 The miser in a play by Plautus entitled *Aulularia* sometimes translated as *The Little Pot* or *The Pot of Gold*.
3 Mentioned in Plautus' *Captivi*.

At this point young Adolphus, no doubt by accident, had turned two pages together, for a gap of two blank pages suddenly interrupted the narrative here.—Then he continued.

"If I had meandered too slowly along the road to Arcueil, or if I had enjoyed for too long the rather uncouth company of my uncle, it happened on a number of occasions that caught out by nightfall and being no longer able to return to Paris without risking some danger, I had to ask for a lodging at the castle. My uncle had always been terrified by this circumstance and had never agreed to offer me this fleeting hospitality except with extreme repugnance and having exhausted all the niceties politeness could imagine to hint to someone that he would do best to leave.

"Finally, when he was convinced of the inefficacity of his expulsive eloquence, of the uselessness of his ingenious efforts to make me change my mind, he would sullenly take me to the spot that was to be my lodging. It was normally an immense loft above the stables, the one on the right of the garden when one enters the main courtyard.

"There, my good uncle, having invited me to enjoy the benefits of sleeping on a heap of dry grass, would wish me good evening and good night, would leave me without light, and would carefully lock the door behind him, so that he kept me prisoner until daylight the next day.

"You can see that the fellow did not have great confidence in his nephew.

"As I would go to bed on an empty stomach, my sleep was not very deep; the cry of an owl taking flight, the slightest murmur of the wind in the tiles, would alert my eyes and my ears.

"One night when I was, I do not know why, very agitated on my bed of fodder, and that I had heard eleven o'clock, midnight, one o'clock in the morning ringing from the village church, I thought I heard someone walking outside.—It was the heavy, loud noise of a human footstep walking in the dark on bare and silent earth.

"I got up, and, moving cautiously in case I bumped into a post or became lost in the roof timbers, I reached a sort of skylight, without frame or glass, which allowed me to sense the perfumed air of the night whilst revealing to me through its narrow opening a small amount of the blue of the sky and a few handfuls of stars.

"I carefully slipped out onto the platform jutting well out from the wall like those one often finds in front of the skylights of hay lofts; I leaned over the handrail around it and could just make out, through the undergrowth and the dense clumps of trees in the garden, a pale glow similar to the light of a lantern. This glow, as far as I could tell as it moved through the foliage, seemed to be following a winding route but which was however getting gradually closer to the castle. If I had not heard at the same time the sand crunch under the soles of shoes, the ground resound with a heavy tread, I would certainly have mistaken this small, bright flame for one of those will-of-the-wisps which flutter at night in the countryside, for one of those little elves or leprechauns who, having stolen the phosphorus from a glow-worm or a firefly, come and place themselves cunningly in front of travellers to make them lose their way and lead them after a thousand roguish tricks, into the depths of a marsh.

"Finally, the light, still moving forward, reached the end of a pathway, carried on along the flowerbeds beside the lawn and went into the sort of forecourt created by the castle and the square formed by the two wings.

"It was then that I clearly recognised my old uncle in his costume of a Carthusian monk that made him look like a veritable ghost.

"He was carrying the lantern whose pale light I had seen from far away in the depths of the park, and which was reflecting on his beard, on the large folds of his robe, for some distance around him, a sort of luminous mist similar to the pale aureole surrounding the disc of the moon when the sky is hazy.

"My uncle crossed the courtyard, heading towards a flight of steps at the corner of the main building, opened a small, low, secret door, painted the same colour as the wall, and, after glancing anxiously around, he went in and disappeared through the thick door.

"I heard the wooden door slam shut, a loud noise of iron and locks, then the sinister noise stopped, and I was alone on the balcony of my dormer window, lost in that profound peace that prevails in the countryside at that hour, alone, with a multitude of thoughts, on one of those beautiful summer nights where the whole of nature seems to have fallen asleep under love's caresses.

"But what the devil had my uncle been doing in the park with his lantern? Like the beautiful Zoraida,[1] who at night would meet a young Moorish knight beneath the white rose bushes of the Alhambra, did he have secret

1 A character in *Don Quixote*.

meetings, under the cover of darkness, under the trees of his garden?

"Was it his habit to tear himself thus from his rest and his sleep to indulge in this sort of mournful stroll, or was it just an outing brought about by chance? The thought intrigued me for a few moments, then I soon forgot this vulgar incident and, with dawn beginning to appear over the horizon and to erase the darkness of night below its pale colour, I went back to stretch myself out on my bed of dry grass on which, this time, I fell deeply asleep.

"Not long after that episode, and with my uncle, from whom I had requested a lodging having, as usual, gallantly locked me in above the stables, there came back to me the memory of the nocturnal scene I have just described.

"I was not feeling very sleepy as I had supped, I think, on two walnuts and a pear and my entrails were crying out with hunger; I said to myself: let's see for certain whether Master Jean, my uncle, spends his nights running in the fields like a tomcat;—I installed myself as best I could on the platform of the dormer window.

"From the top of my watchtower, like a night watchman in a war-torn city, I could see the countryside all around, I was overlooking everything around me, the garden, the buildings, the park, it was impossible to enter or leave the castle without being seen by me.

"It was certainly wrong, what I was doing there; it was very indiscreet. Ah! Why did I not suppress this first onset of a guilty curiosity! I would not have been led to do what I did subsequently, I would not be here today stretched out on these flagstones, with no hope other than in death, which will no doubt be slow to come and very reluctant.

"At around midnight, my uncle Jean came carefully out through the small, low door through which I had seen him go in on the famous night of my discovery. Just like the first time he was carrying a lantern; he crossed the courtyard in the same way, reached the garden and the park, seeming to take exactly the same route only this time in reverse. Then as the glow of the lantern moved deeper and deeper into the thickness of the coppice, I soon saw nothing more, I lost all trace. Noise, shadow and light, all had disappeared.

"Good Lord! I cried, even if my uncle is not in the first flush of youth, he is certainly reliable! And the lady waiting for him every night in the foliage, could not but be very charmed by his timekeeping; for ladies like nothing more than to find in their lovers the virtues that make good servants! A lover, he is the lackey of a heart.

"And as far as lackeys are concerned, I was the lackey of my curiosity and I waited patiently at my dormer window for the return of my uncle, rather like a sedan chair porter waiting at the door of a private house.

"Ah! When one goes wenching, time has light wings. However, the fellow was not forgetting himself in his happiness; and as one o'clock in the morning was striking, I saw him appear straightaway or rather, I should say, I saw the light of his lantern: does love ever move forward without a burning torch!

"But it is not right for me to amuse myself with such badinage. My uncle, such an anchorite, so breathless and so past it, to be passing his time with love affairs! The poor man! Ah! Would to heaven a thousand times that he had been going to serenade his sweetheart!

"As he was slowly coming back into the corner of the courtyard and reaching the low door on the staircase, my uncle genuinely had the funereal look of an inhabitant of the Styx or of an old gnome going off to sup with the dead.

"I wished him *bon appétit* and returned to snuggle down on my bed of hay. But I nevertheless swore that I would succeed in discovering the motive for the nocturnal excursions of my uncle. In addition, my imagination was piqued.

"As a result, in Paris I had a silken ladder of about six cubits[1] made. The maker thought that I was planning to use it for some amorous enterprise; I allowed him to maintain this belief and I confess that my romantic mood was infinitely flattered.

"Yesterday during the day, when I had taken possession of this audacious instrument that could have helped me make such agreeable amorous ascensions, I rolled it round by body, under my doublet, so as to hide it as best I could from the penetrating gaze of Master Jean, and I came to seek lodgings at the castle. In order to motivate my visit, I brought a few skeins of thread and some needles that my uncle had asked me for.

"At the regular time for his exit, just as midnight was striking, the low door opened and my uncle, carrying his lantern, began to make his way as normal in the direction of the park.

"Quickly I threw out my ladder that had been ready for a while, and once I had fastened it to the balcony of my dormer window, I hast-

---

1 The distance from the elbow to the fingertips.

ily climbed down, so quickly that I might have made a squirrel die of envy.

"I ran quietly in the direction of the light, and on tiptoes I reached Master Jean d'Anspach just as he was about to go into a clump of trees in the park.

"For fear of giving myself away, I kept my distance. I hid behind the trunk of a huge beech tree and, staring into the darkness through the foliage and the lattice of the branches, I tried to work out what activity my uncle could possibly have in this place. The story of Muma Pompilius[1] and his muse came to mind; but today nymphs are rarer, and especially their sweet words.

"I first of all saw my dear uncle bend over, put down his lantern beside him, and make a thick pile of twigs and dead leaves; then I saw him laboriously lift the heavy flap of a trapdoor level with the ground, having pulled back the bolts; next I saw him throw it aside on the pile of twigs and leaves, pick up his lantern, and gradually disappear into the void left by the trapdoor, seeming to sink into the ground by degrees as if he had gone down the steps of an underground staircase.

"I carefully went up to the opening, I risked a timid glance, and I saw below me, at the bot-

---

1 The legendary second King of Rome after Romulus.

tom of a long sequence of stone steps carved out between the two walls of a narrow corridor, the emaciated silhouette of my uncle who was moving forward hunched over in a space that was so dark that my eye could scarcely follow him.

"Then I saw him sink again into the ground; gradually he disappeared, as if the earth had fled from his forked foot, but still leaving after his total disappearance a feeble glow of light, becoming ever weaker, similar to the trace of phosphorus and sulphur left by Lucifer, but which soon went out completely.

"I waited for a few moments, my ears pricked up, my eyes turned in the same direction; but hearing nothing more and not seeing the light reappear, I slipped into the staircase, ready to risk breaking my neck, for I was longing to know what my uncle could be celebrating at the bottom of this well.

"I reached the foot of the stairs unhindered, and after taking a few steps on a flat surface, I found myself on the edge of the orifice through which Master Jean had disappeared. I leaned over the ventilation shaft, I saw at the bottom of a spiral staircase a weak and slowly moving light which, turning round several times on itself, had just died at my feet. Led by this light, I went down this narrow spiral again, step by step, and I suddenly arrived in the bare, vaulted room which precedes this one.

"My uncle was now in this last cell. There, next to him, on a large chest, was placed this little iron lamp which is giving me light now and allowing me to write these few lines. But let us make haste, in vain do I tip it, I can only see a few drops of oil left in the reservoir; the wick, which I am continually raising, has almost reached its limit; and when the light leaves this lamp, it will also for ever leave my eyelid. Alas! Oh, my uncle, we must die! What a desperate and cruel end! But already the old man cannot hear me. His cold, clenched hand no longer responds when I touch him with mine. Farewell, farewell, my uncle! Oh! Say that you forgive me!

"But if, instead of remaining idle and resigned, I were to call out, to shake these bars continuously! If I gnawed away at this grill with my teeth? . . . Call out! . . . in this isolated and lonely place, in this subterranean depth, who could hear my cries and bring me help? . . . In vain would I dry my voice up in my throat, in vain would I grind down my teeth on the iron.

"As my uncle had his back turned to the entrance, I could not see what was keeping him motionless in the same pose. He seemed to me, however, to be looking at something carefully, in a sort of absorption or ecstasy. He had so much love, the poor man, so much love for his golden calf!

"The door to the cellar was wide open; crazily, stupidly, without thinking about what I was doing, about the terror, the surprise that my unannounced presence could create in this place, giving in to childishness, I crossed the threshold, I moved quietly towards my uncle. But when I was close to him, walking on tip-toes, I tripped, lost my balance and, trying to regain it, put my heel down too noisily on the floor.

"At this noise, my uncle turned round in an indescribable terror and, recognising me immediately, he gave me a flaming, threatening look.

"He had placed himself in front of his barrels and chests, that I had seen were full of gold, like a lioness protecting her cubs.

"Then rushing at me in a rage (he had become deranged by anger and terror) he came, the old fellow, to throw himself or rather break himself on my chest. If I had not held him up, I think that as a result of his own shock he would have measured his length backwards on the flagstones.

"I do not know whether he mistook this gesture I was making to help him; but, trembling like a leaf, 'Wretch!' he screamed at me in an exhausted voice. 'You come to rob me and to kill me! Well then! Die with me!'—And in his folly, lost in his own rage and his own threats, he violently pushed the grill closed behind me.

"But scarcely had he made this gesture than, letting out a long cry of regret and despair, he tried to undo what he had done; but the latches and the springs had already banged shut in their lockets. It was too late.

"Motionless and frozen, downcast like a valet at the sight of a vase that has slipped from his hands and has broken, the old man remained there, devastated, crushed.

"Whatever one tried to do, the door could only be opened from outside.

"We were for ever sealed in the tomb.

"I still have many things to say; but it is getting darker and darker. The wick is only giving off a weak, red light; it is flickering, it is smoking, it is going out! How many horrible hours still await me here! I can no longer see, I do not know what I am writing . . . Oh you, my reader, turn your gaze away from my misfortune! Oh! Just say a prayer or shed a tear for me!"

There followed a few more words, but they were completely illegible.

Then, by chance, much further on and lost among a few blank pages of the notebook, M. d'Argenson found this written in large letters and completely out of order. It was necessary to guess rather than to read:

"I only have my imagination and my suffering to measure time. Perhaps I have already been here for a few days locked in this dungeon, tortured by hunger,—what a horrible ordeal!

"In my chest I seem to have a crowd of devouring animals that are gnawing on it and grinding it at their pleasure.

"My jaws are becoming tense and are clenching; I cannot say a word.

"I am so exhausted that my fingers cannot hold the pencil that I have just picked up to try to write a few more sentences despite the darkness.

"Oh my God, when will thought leave me as well as life!

"O my God, how I am suffering! . . ."

The pencil had then left nothing more than a shapeless mark, as if the trembling, exhausted hand had moved across the paper, dragged by its own weight.

We may believe that poor Adolphus did not survive long after this last effort.

When M. Voyer d'Argenson had finished deciphering these last words, the last lament of the unfortunate nephew of Master Jean d'Anspach, Suzanne, who had noticed the different impressions that had been seen on his face from time to time, said to him with a smile: "What are you reading there that is so terrible, for you are quite moved Monseigneur?"

"I am reading, my beautiful prophetess, a terrible story full of anguish and death, a story of people starved to death, and who nevertheless were not frequent travellers to Mount Helicon."[1]

---

1 In Greek mythology Mount Helicon was supposed to be the source of poetic inspiration.

XVIII

IT was only in the afternoon that the courier sent by the King to M. d'Argenson returned.

Just over eight hours had passed between his departure and his return, and these eight hours that, in the opinion of the Lieutenant-General, had passed too quickly seemed to him to be nothing more than a few enjoyable moments spent in delightful company.

It is true that, once he had finished reading the notebook of the unfortunate nephew of Master Jean, he had fallen at the feet of his captive and had not stopped surrounding her with the most diligent care, giving her all the signs of admiration and sympathy that can only be imagined by the most refined courtesy.

Suzanne had gradually given up her original harshness; she was listening to the gallant words and the evident affection of her admirer in a rather less disdainful manner; she had no doubt felt that she had more to lose than to gain by being rebellious.—It is so easy for beauty to change its chains into garlands of flowers.

One part of the morning had thus passed delicately in the joyful banter and in the expansive pleasures of the table; nothing is more favourable to sweet talk and for mind games. M. d'Argenson had had improvised a very agreeable, pleasant lunch, a surprisingly sumptuous one since it had only comprised the culinary resources of a village.

How could Suzanne have resisted such pleasant manners, such noble attentions? This last detail, by that I mean the lunch, had especially contributed to convert our cruel lady.

The reply from the King brought by the messenger was brief and to the point.

"A good catch!" His Majesty said. "Have all the gold-seekers put in jail, and all this gold put in my treasury; it will help to pay for the board and lodging of our magicians and will subsidise the expenses of the new war that I am preparing.—The business will remain a secret. Leave the bodies in their natural tomb, and have the den filled in so that henceforth there is no mention of it."

Armed with the sovereign's order the Lieutenant-General did not hesitate to come to our apartment where, since he had kept us imprisoned, he had only made a few short visits. It was obvious, we had lost the best part of ourselves; he had taken from us the only pearl which shone on our foreheads, the only perfume that wafted among us; he had taken away our Suzanne! Suzanne was with him, Suzanne overwhelmed him, fascinated him, intoxicated him, immobilised him . . . Ah! Who would willingly exchange the sweet rays that emanate from a star for a stupid, desolate atmosphere?

Mind you, we had not remained entirely tearful; no, thanks to our reverend prior, a man full of stratagems in such matters, and to the helpfulness of the owner of the castle who was a prisoner like us, a prisoner in his own home, we had also managed to improvise a substantial lunch, but one without glory: Suzanne was not there. Even Bacchus would have been in mourning. I certainly know that, where I was concerned, if I had not feared making my mistake more serious and worsening my position, I would have declared myself openly to be the rival of the Lieutenant-General, and, with my sword in my hand, I would have claimed our Helen.

"Gentlemen," M. d'Argenson said to us, pretending to feel a sharp sense of regret (this air of regret is part and parcel of the apparatus of a magistrate), "I have received the orders from his Majesty that I was waiting for, they are, as I predicted, very precise and very severe; but count on my benevolence, on the goodwill I bear you; I shall do all I can to alleviate the consequences of his royal anger. Believe me that, were it in my power, this affair would not have unpleasant consequences."

Lies and hypocrisy! One hour after this fine speech, without care for our rank or nobility, we were piled into a covered cart, no doubt borrowed from some farmer in the village, and without telling us where we were going, we were taken away with a large escort of mounted police.

As the sun was reaching the horizon and the earth was beginning to cover itself with the veil of evening, we reached the wood and the jail of Vincennes.

I leave you to imagine our terror and stupor when we saw ourselves dragged into this state prison.

XIX

IN the very night following this transfer, that is to say during the first night of sadness and horror that we spent in Vincennes in our genuine cells, the gold and all the riches hidden in the cellar of Master Jean d'Anspach were removed and placed in the treasury of the King.

The following night, according to the desire of his Majesty, the underground halls that the old usurer had had constructed with so much care and at so much expense were closed and filled with earth and all sorts of debris, right up to the top of the opening; so much so that all traces of it have disappeared and it would be exceedingly difficult to indicate today where it was.

The first act of the chief jailer was not a generous one; he separated me from my companions in misfortune who were, no doubt, also separated from one another. I never saw them again and have no idea what happened to them.

Where Suzanne is concerned, no doubt thanks to her beauty, she was not locked away in Vincennes. It is even said that M. d'Argenson had spoken about her to the King in such gallant terms that the monarch, whose aversion for magicians had probably greatly decreased since his coffers had been increased at their expense, wanted her to come to Versailles, where she did appear in the fine costume of a soothsayer, the one that she was wearing the day we were arrested in front of the cavern.— What became of this visit to the court and the affection of the Lieutenant-General, that is a long and amorous story, that here is not the place to recount.

Besides there isn't enough time for that today, added M. de Brederode; Dijon, our fine jailer, is there waiting for us and becoming impatient.

Dijon don't get angry, we are all yours, we are following you.

XX

THERE you have, as we said at the beginning of this work about M. de Brederode,
the strange fable that this Dutch gentleman
normally told his companions in captivity.

Could it be the truth, pure and simple, as
we have already said? Could it be an invention
of his mind disturbed by a too long incarceration, a fiction that he had concocted to disguise
the real reason for his imprisonment, which
perhaps was not one of those that can easily
be confessed? We do not know, and we repeat,
since the archives of the Bastille are totally silent on this matter, it is probable that we shall
never know.

What is indisputable is that the poor captive,
whose behaviour was gentle and peaceful, after
two years in Vincennes spent a further twelve
years in the Bastille, and that, at the end of this

life imprisonment, worn out by boredom and sorrow, he fell ill, and so gravely, that he had to be transported to hospital where the death he had called for so often finally brought an end his suffering.

What is no less certain is that the belief in a treasure, still there but hidden, Lord knows where, in the land around the village of Arcueil, lasts to this day. If the police and the King, in the first days of the eighteenth century, actually did remove it, this removal must have been done very secretly for, since that time, popular opinion has not changed.

I myself have seen in Arcueil, in a property divided and broken up by speculators, a sort of entrance to an icehouse that was said to be the external orifice of an unknown, impenetrable, underground room supposed to contain an immense treasure:

The treasure of Master Jean d'Anspach!

GOTTFRIED WOLFGANG

Life is nothing more than the dream of a shadow.
PINDAR[1]

---

1 A Greek lyric poet who died in 438 BCE.

TONY:

I'll tell you more, there was a fish taken,
A monstrous fish, with a sword by's side, a long sword.
A pike in's neck and a gun in's nose, a huge gun,
And letters of mast in's mouth from the duke of
Florence.

CLEANTHE:

This (is?) a monstrous lie.

TONY:

I do confess it.
Do you think I'd tell you truths?

(Fletcher's *Wife for a Month*)[1]

---

1 Borel ascribes this dialogue in English in the text to
John Fletcher's *A Wife for a Month* first performed in
1624. In reality it is taken from *The Mad Lover* performed
around 1616-1617. *A Wife for a Month* was published in
the Beaumont and Fletcher first folio in 1647. *The Mad
Lover* was published in the second folio in 1679. Borel
did read English and had, in fact, translated *Robinson
Crusoe* into French.

I

I had been in Boulogne for some time and shortly before I was due to leave my landlord approached me courteously and offering me a fairly voluminous bundle of papers:

"Please allow me Sir," he said, "to offer you these, you will no doubt be able to make better use of them than I can. A young, very taciturn and very strange Englishman was lodging here: that was about two years ago . . . One evening, he went out; he was seen heading for the jetty, and since that time there has been no trace of him nor have I had any news of him. I have kept all these papers as well as all his luggage, of which there is not very much, almost nothing in fact . . . Alas! This poor young man spent all his days and all his nights thinking and writing!"

The so cruel end of this young foreigner who, like so many others, had no doubt dreamed of a very gentle death after a career full of glory and happiness . . . this pain, so isolated and so obscure, of which only the sea's waves where it had been extinguished knew the secret, had moved me greatly; I was prey to a painful emotion; I locked myself in my room and, my soul full of discouragement, I began avidly to read the papers that had been entrusted to me, the last sad remains of an intelligence that had succumbed without a struggle!—lost without chance of return, obliterated! I told myself: at least if it were possible to save one of these pages from oblivion, it would be a consolation for the shadow of this unfortunate young man, who is doubtless there, wandering around me, considering me very brazen to be touching his remains! . . .

In the middle of a heap of scarcely started poems, amidst all sorts of unconnected and unfinished fragments, but always imbued with a certain character of grandeur and superstition, I soon found a small exercise book, with neither date nor title, in which was written in an almost illegible hand the strange story that follows.

Was this curious composition the work of this poor unknown man? Was it simply a copy or a translation that he had made of some phantasmagorical piece that had flowered in the misty brain of a German, or which he had found in France and that had appealed to his sickly mind? I do not know . . . fate has put it in my hands; as fate has given it to me, so do I transmit it.—Let the crazy person to whom this could belong, make himself known!—And, if so, immediately he will receive compensation.

II

IT was at the time of the French Revolution. On a stormy night, at the hour that is often called unreasonable, a young German was walking through the old districts of Paris and was making his way silently to his dwelling. Flashes of lightning were blinding his eyes, the noise of thunder, the storm's violence echoed in the twisting streets of the old city . . . But allow me, please, to tell you something about my young Saxon.

Gottfried Wolfgang was a young man of good family. For a time, he had studied at Göttingen; but being visionary and passionate, he had indulged in those speculative doctrines that so frequently have led German youth astray. The withdrawn life that he led, his constant diligence and the singular nature of his studies had gradually impaired his moral and physical faculties. His health was undermined, his imagination sick. He had pushed his abstract daydreams about spiritual essences so far that he had ended up by creating for himself, like Swedenborg,[1] an ideal world gravitating around him; and he had convinced himself, in his folly, that a malign influence, an evil spirit was always hovering above his head, waiting for the chance to kill him. Such a crazy idea, acting on his already melancholic, idiosyncratic nature, had resulted in the most deplorable effects. Since he had become shy and had succumbed to the bleakest discouragement, the mental illness of which he was in the grip quickly manifested itself; and because a change of scenery had seemed to be the most effective remedy for his cruel situation, he had been sent to finish his studies amidst the splendours and the whirlwind of Paris.

Just as Wolfgang arrived in the capital, the first disorders of the Revolution were breaking out. At first his exhilarated mind, captivated by the political and philosophical theories of the time, had paid its tribute to the popular frenzy. But since the bloody scenes that had followed had wounded his sensitive nature, had

---

1 Emmanuel Swedenborg (1688-1772) was a Swedish theologian.

disgusted him with society and the world, and had soon restored him to his monastic habits, he had withdrawn to a small, solitary lodging, chosen in a dark street, not far from the old Sorbonne, in the centre of the Latin Quarter. Once installed there Wolfgang had once again given free reign to his favourite speculations. If occasionally he ventured out of his dear cell, it was only to go and lock himself away for whole days in the great depositories of books in Paris, these catacombs of light-headed authors, the underground Romes of thought, where he delved enthusiastically, seeking nourishment to satisfy his sickly mind, into the dustiest of books, the most out-dated books of spells. Our student was in some way (please excuse me this slight lack of taste) a sort of literary vampire gorging himself on the mass grave of dead science and of the last remains of literature.

Despite his liking for the solitary life, Gottfried had an ardent and sensual temperament, which normally scarcely manifested itself except in his mind. He was too shy and too innocent to have a love life; but at the same time, he confessed that he was a passionate admirer of beauty. Often, he would lose himself in endless dreams about faces or shapes he had seen, and his imagination created for him idols that it adorned with perfections by far surpassing all reality.

At the time when his brain was in this state of over-excitement, he had a dream that affected him in an extraordinary way. The vision had been of a woman of transcendent beauty and the impression that this image had made on him was so strong that he saw it constantly, at all times and in every place; day and night his brain was full of it. Finally, he was so infatuated with this illusion, and this craziness had lasted so long, that it had turned into one of those *idées fixes* that is sometimes confused, where melancholic men are concerned, with madness.

Let us pick up the story that we interrupted earlier and let us follow our young German in his night-time walk. As he was crossing the Place de Grève he suddenly found himself close to the g . . . No, never will my pen be able to write this hideous word . . . He stepped back in horror . . . It was at the height of the Terror. Therefore, this horrible instrument was there permanently and the purest and the most innocent blood gushed onto the scaffold. This very day it had been used for some act of carnage and was still presenting, as it waited for new victims, its lugubrious and threatening apparatus to the sleeping city.

Wolfgang felt himself fainting and he was turning away trembling when he suddenly noticed a mysterious person, crouching, so to speak, at the foot of the scaffold. A succession of quick flashes of lightning soon made the outline more distinct to the student's eyes: it was a woman, dressed entirely in black, appearing to belong to the upper class. More than one beautiful head that was used to resting on down pillows now rested on stone in these times of awful hardships. She was sitting on the lowest step, her body leaning forward and her face hidden in her lap. Her long, thick hair came down to the ground, letting drip like a thatched roof the torrential rain that was falling. Wolfgang stopped short in front of this solitary monument of misfortune:

"Perhaps," he told himself, "from the shore of existence where this unfortunate woman lies with a broken heart, the terrible blade has sent to eternity all that was dear to her in the world." Propelled by an irresistible power he stepped forward in a timid and embarrassed fashion and addressed a few sympathetic words to the woman who was arousing in him so much pity and so much interest. She raised her head and stared at him with a bewildered look. But imagine the astonishment of Wolfgang as he recognised in the brilliant light of the flashes of lightning the reality whose shadow had for so long subjugated all his faculties. The face of the unknown woman, although deathly white at the moment, and bearing a mark of deep despair, was ravishingly beautiful.

The most violent and diverse emotions were stirring the passionate heart of Wolfgang. Trembling, he spoke to her again. He was surprised to see her out on her own at such an hour, in such a place, subject to the fury of the storm, and he ended up graciously offering to take her safely to her family or to her friends. But she, with a horribly significant gesture, and a voice that strangely impressed her interlocutor, replied "I have no friends on this earth."

"But you have perhaps a shelter?"

"Yes, in the grave!"

Gottfried's soul was shattered.

"If a simple student," he continued with a modest hesitation, "were able, without the fear of being misunderstood, to offer his humble abode for shelter and his arm for protection . . . I am a foreigner here in France and, just like you, without friends in this city; but if my life can be of service to you, it is at your disposal and would be sacrificed before any harm or the slightest insult could touch you!"

There was in the manner of the young man an honest eagerness which had its effect. True enthusiasm possesses a particular elegance about which there can be no mistake. The woman from the scaffold entrusted herself implicitly to Gottfried's protection.

The storm had become less intense, the noise of the thunder was now only in the distance. The whole of Paris was still at rest, the great volcano of human passions was sleeping for a few moments in order to gather together new forces for the eruption of the following day.

Our two heroes walked together for more than an hour: Gottfried was supporting the faltering footsteps of his companion and both of them kept a strict silence. Finally, when they had walked along the dark walls of the Sorbonne, they arrived at the end of their journey at the narrow old hovel, the abode of the student.—Wolfgang, the monk, in the company of a woman! At this extraordinary sight, the old concierge who had got out of bed to open up, was struck by indescribable astonishment.

As he was going into his lodging, our young German blushed for the first time at its miserable appearance. He only had one room, in truth one that was quite big, but encumbered with the normal clutter of the student; the bed was in a deep alcove at one end of the room.

Gottfried could now look at his companion in a more leisurely way. He felt himself more than ever intoxicated with her beauty. Her complexion, of a dazzling whiteness, was as though set off by a profusion of jet-black hair which floated casually on the ivory of her shoulders. Her eyes were large and shining; but, in their expression, something haggard could be seen. Her waist, as far as the black clothing allowed one to judge, was perfect. She looked extremely noble and distinguished despite the simplicity of her outfit. The only thing she was wearing that had any appearance of luxury or finery was a wide black velvet choker, a sort of cravat held together by diamond clasps.

However, the student was slightly embarrassed about how to put decorously into practice the hospitality he was offering to the unfortunate being he was protecting. He even thought of letting her have the room to herself and going off to find a different shelter for himself; but he was so fascinated, his mind and his senses were in thrall to such a powerful charm that he could not tear himself away from her presence. Moreover, the behaviour of the unknown woman was contributing to holding him back. She seemed to have forgotten her pain and the terrible circumstances to which

Wolfgang owed his encounter with her. The love and care of the young man, having won her confidence, had also apparently won her heart.

In the intoxication of the moment Wolfgang told her he was passionately in love with her. He recounted his mysterious dreams; he told her how she had possessed his heart before he had ever seen her. Strangely agitated as he was talking to her, in her turn she confessed that she felt drawn towards him by an almost supernatural compulsion.

"Then why should we ever separate?" cried Wolfgang at the height of his delirium, "our hearts are united by a power of attraction; in the eyes of reason and of honour; we are just one single being . . . Do we have need of vulgar formulas to bind together our two great souls!"

The woman with the black choker was listening carefully and with an ever-increasing attention.

"You have neither lodging nor family," continued Wolfgang, "well, let me be everything for you, or rather let us be everything each one for the other! Here is my hand, I commit myself to you for ever."

"For ever?" she said, solemnly.

"For ever," Wolfgang affirmed.

The stranger took hold of the hand he was offering her.

"So, I am yours, for ever," she murmured.

As she spoke these last words, she gave her lover a long look, full of melancholy and tenderness.

The following morning Gottfried went out early to look for a larger and more appropriate apartment now that his personal circumstances had changed. He had left his fiancée peacefully asleep. When he came back, he found her still deeply asleep, but her head was lolling out of the large armchair in which she had wanted to spend the night, modestly wrapped up in a blanket. One of her arms was resting on her forehead in a strange way. He spoke to her but there was no reply. He stepped forward to wake her up and to stop her lying in this uncomfortable and dangerous position; but her hand was cold; but she had no pulse, but her face was pale and contracted . . . She was dead!!!

Distraught, terrified, Gottfried lets out shrill cries. The whole neighbourhood arrives;—the scene is heart-breaking . . .

Summoned by the concierge a policeman arrives; but as he goes into the room and sees the body, he steps back in horror . . .

"Good God," he cries, "how come this woman is here?"

"So, do you know her?" poor Gottfried asks quickly.

"Do I know her!" replies the officer. "I! . . . this woman! . . . Yesterday she died on the scaffold!"

Upon these words, quicker than a thunderbolt, Wolfgang steps forward and unties the black band that surrounds the so beautiful neck of his fiancée.

And immediately he is confronted with the sight of the horrible and bloody traces of the fatal knife!!!

"Horror! Horror!" he cries, in a growing outburst of delirium. "Oh, I see it well, the evil genius has taken possession of me, I am lost for ever. My enemy has brought this body back to life to set a cruel trap for me and I have fallen into it. What a terrible anti-climax . . ."

III

THE improbability of this story, some details of which must no doubt have shocked some readers, will be accounted for in a quite natural way when we have said that Gottfried Wolfgang, a little time after this vision that he so often liked to recount, died in a lunatic asylum.